Praise for JULIUS FAST'S
BODY LANGUAGE

"A brightly readable, enlightening and perceptively amusing book."
—*Publishers Weekly*

"Fast has written a book that can be a valuable aid in heightening our awareness of ourselves and others."
—*Journal of Emotional Education*

"A very fascinating explanation of nonverbal communication."
—*American Association for the Advancement of Science*

"Fast's book should definitely be read by professionals who work with people."
—*Bestsellers*

"Fast's book is . . . actually a crash course in sensitivity."
—*Saturday Review*

"Full of unexpected revelations and gems of insight."
—*Dr. David Reuben*

5 months on the New York Times Bestseller List!

We will send you a free catalog on request. Any titles not in your local book store can be purchased by mail. Send the price of the book plus 50 cents shipping charge to Tower Books, P.O. Box 270, Norwalk, Connecticut 06852.

Titles currently in print are available for industrial and sales promotion at reduced rates. Address inquiries to Tower Publications, Inc., Two Park Avenue, New York, New York 10016, Attention: Premium Sales Department.

BODY
POLITICS

How to Get Power with Class

Julius Fast

TOWER BOOKS NEW YORK CITY

For
Julia Laura

A TOWER BOOK

Published by

Tower Publications, Inc.
Two Park Avenue
New York, N.Y. 10016

Contents

Introduction   7

1. OBNOXIOUS POWER   14

Oliver's Ordeal. The Power Players. The Gentle
Seduction. The Gentle Touch. Martyr Power.
Klutzing Out. The Potency of Impotence.
Those Dirty Little Games

2. FINDING YOUR POWER PROFILE   43

The Unhappy Chairman. Power Profiles. The
Corruption of Power. Interior vs. Exterior. The
Apartment. The Vacation. The Passing Years.
Love and Marriage. And Now the Kids. What
Kind of Person Am I? The Dominance Quot-
ient. The Conversation. Chow Time. On the
Job. The Lovers. Who Dominates Whom?
Aggression or Assertiveness. The Movie Line.
The Waiter with the Water. The New Neigh-
bors. The Bus Ride. The Roadhog. Scoring
Your Aggression. Wearing the Leadership
Mantle. The Boss. The Method. The Order.
The Risk. A Job Well Done. Your Score.
Prescott's Problem. Tommy's Takeover.

3. THE SOURCES OF POWER   74

Verbal Games. Dr. Hunt's Experiments.
Table Politics. The Wonder Child. The Baby
Tug-of-War. Legitimate and Coercive Power.
Reward Power and Group Power. The Power
of Responsibility.

4. WOMAN POWER   99

The Shift in the Family. Sarah's Scenario.
You Scratch My Back—I'll Scratch Yours.
The Expert Technique. Power by Identifica-
tion. The Impotent Tycoon. The Fear of
Power.

5. THE BODY LANGUAGE OF POWER   124

A Ride on the New York Subways. A Ques-
tion of Feedback. Handling Space. Building
Personal Power. The World of Touch.
Speaking of Power. The Family Dictator.

6. RISKING   153

Nothing Ventured, Nothing Gained. Risking
Intimacy. The Fear of Risking. Your Inner
Risk Factor. Learning to Risk.

7. COPING WITH POWER   173

A Little Stress Never Hurts. Exercising Your
Assertion Muscles. The Flexible Woman.
The Three Sides of Reason. Stepping Back
to Look Closer. The Sensitive Salesman. Putting It All Together.

8. IMAGE PROJECTION   193

Dressing for Dinner. By Their Clothes You
Shall Know Them. Dressing Down. The
Corporate Image. The Masks We Wear. The
Hired Brain.

9. THE POWER PACKAGE   213

Packaging People. Looking Out for You-
Know-Who.

Epilogue: POWER WITH CLASS   218

Creative Power. Risks, Stress and Reason.

Introduction

POWER: How To Misuse It

I ran into my friend, Alvin, the other day, and after our "Hello's," "How have you been's?" and all that, I asked "How have you *really* been?"

Shaking his head sorrowfully, Alvin said, "Just awful. I screwed up on a job interview last week, and believe me, I wanted that job so badly I could taste it."

"Doing what?"

"Designing ratchets for Silverman's."

"Silverman's?"

"You know that big outfit. Silverman's Cooperative Ratchet Engineering Works. Well, I've worked with ratchets all my life, and I've got ideas about their design that would revolutionize the industry. I finally wrangled an interview with Sam Chelsea, one of their top executives—and I blew it."

I took him into a nearby bar and over a couple of beers I listened to his story.

"I really wanted to have everything go well with this interview," he explained, "so I decided to do my homework first."

"What do you mean?" I frowned. "You mean

you studied up on ratchets?''

"Hell, no, I know my ratchets. I studied up on how to get a job."

"But if your job was designing ratchets . . ."

"Hey, man, where have you been? What counts in today's job market is power and how to use it. It's all a duel for power, and there are definite ways to play the game."

"I never thought of it as a game."

"Well, it is. The most dangerous game of all. I've studied up on this, *Power Through Clothes, Looking Out For Yourself, Success and How to Get There.* I read all the books, and then I dressed the part."

Fascinated, I downed my beer and ordered another. "Tell me how you dressed the part."

"First, I made sure my suit was perfectly tailored, the jacket flat across my shoulder blades, the sleeves five inches above the tips of my thumbs, the top trouser button just covering my navel—oh, it fit like a dream, and I selected just the right suit."

"What was that?"

"I wanted to appear conservative, send a message of understated firmness, a man the company could trust, yet someone who could do great things."

I shook my head in wonder. "How did you manage that?"

"A single-breasted suit with a vest, an understated pattern in grey flannel, a crisp white shirt."

Fascinated, I asked, "What about cuffs?"

"Cuffs?"

"You know, on your trousers."

"Oh. No cuffs. They break the visual line of a

long leg. You never use them in business suits."

"And a white shirt."

"Well, I considered pin stripes, very narrow pin stripes, but I finally decided against them. The books say that solid, pale colors are safest, and white is always good. It spells dignity, strength."

"I see."

"And I went all out with a silk tie, expensive, but there's power to silk. A tiny, all-over pattern in blue on blue."

"And shoes?"

"Oh, I was right, even there. A black wingtip oxford and navy blue socks to complement my tie—not match it, get it?"

"I get the picture."

"Hey, it was a fantastic picture. I looked at myself in the mirror and I smelled success, power—even my jewelry was right, a gold wedding band and a plain gold watch, nothing else."

"But Alvin, you're not married."

"Doesn't matter. It's the power look."

"Looking like that . . . my God, how could you blow it?"

His excitement faded, and he looked moodily into his empty glass. "Sam Chelsea, the executive who interviewed me. He's got the controlling interest in the company. I walk into his office, and what do you think he's wearing?"

"I think I get it. The same outfit? Or dressed for more power?"

"Hell, no. Dress for power, my ass! He's wearing sneakers and jeans and a goddamned T-shirt."

"No!"

"Yes! And he's swinging a golf club. He kept playing with that golf club during the whole interview. Look, I adopted what they call the position of power when we sat down."

"What's that?" I asked, intrigued.

"A firm seat. I sat erect and quiet. Fidgeting betrays an inner weakness, so I sat motionless, my eyes fixed on his in a clear, calm gaze. It's always supposed to work."

"But it didn't?"

"He kept fidgeting with that goddamned golf club, tapping his fingers and scratching his nose. Finally he asked me, 'Hey, you got something wrong with you?' and I said, 'No. Why?' and he said, 'You sit so still. Do you have a muscle condition?' It threw me right off balance. Then there was the business with the desk."

"What was that?"

"Well, you know, the desk's a power symbol. His chair was behind the desk, and the one he told me to sit in was in front of the desk."

"Why was the desk a power symbol?"

"Well, man, it was between us. I couldn't let it protect him like that, so I moved my chair cater-corner to his, so there was only the edge of the desk between us."

"What happened?"

Alvin threw up his hands. "He got up and paced around his office swinging that mother of a golf club. When I left, he put his arm around my shoulder, told me he wasn't sure I'd be happy with them, but that I should leave my designs and he'd pass them on. Then he asked me if I'd ever considered floor-walking as a career. What a blow!"

I managed not to choke on my beer, and finally I asked, "What now?"

"Well, I've picked up this book on success

through intimidation. This time I might try a navy blue suit and maybe a maroon silk tie . . ."

Poor Alvin. He's got a long, hard struggle ahead of him and the hell of it is, he knows his ratchets. What he doesn't know is the meaning of power, what it is and what it can do and can't do. Saddest of all, he doesn't know the difference between the outer and the inner trappings of power.

Alvin's problem was a lack of understanding of what power is. It's true, he had no real idea of how to use it, but trying to use power is useless if you don't know what power means. A barrel of books have been written about the use of power to get ahead in the world, and like Alvin, they all seem to concern themselves with the outer trappings of power. In a book about dressing for power, Alvin read that powerful men dress in a very special way. They have their clothes made by the most expensive tailors. They wear certain shoes, certain ties, talk in an assertive way and even sit in a "position of power."

The only truth in the book, of course, is that some powerful men can afford the very best in suits, shirts, ties and shoes—or can afford to get the very best advice in choosing them. However, Alvin had it all backwards. Clothes, gestures and appearances do not get you power. It is power that gets you all these goodies—if you want them.

It was Alvin's disconcerting misfortune to come up against one of those rare men who are uninterested in the trappings of power. Sam Chelsea had enough power to disregard all outward appearances. He had the power to dress as he pleased and act as he pleased. There is no way to

11

play any of the accepted "power games" with a man like that. You are the loser even before the cards are dealt.

The only power Alvin had was his knowledge of ratchets. He was a top man in his field, and this should have given him enough power to be considered for the job. In fact, it eventually did. His designs were passed on by Sam Chelsea to the engineering department, but with no particular recommendation one way or the other. Eventually they were examined by someone who understood their value, and Alvin was called back for another interview.

"Forget everything you've ever read about power or intimidation," I told him when he showed me the letter inviting him to discuss his designs.

"Are you sure you don't think I should try a navy blue suit and a maroon tie? A silk maroon tie?" he asked anxiously.

"Alvin, do you want the job?"

"You know I do!"

"Are you good in your field?"

"Tops. Why do you think they called me back?"

"Then take some advice from an old pro. Sell all your books on power, on winning through intimidation, on creative aggression and all the games people play. I know a good secondhand book store where they'll give you top money for them."

He looked bewildered.

"Like thousands of other people, you've misinterpreted what they've said. You've stood it all on its head. Now take my advice. Sell your books and use the money to buy some clothes bags and moth balls."

"What for?"

"To put away your power clothes. Look, dress the way you always dress, the way you feel most comfortable, and when you go for this second interview forget that position you take on jockeying for power. All those power tricks, if they work, will only antagonize the man who interviews you. Whoever he is, he has more power than you have, and don't ever forget it. Let him have it. The more power he has, the better he'll feel towards you. You concentrate on one thing—your knowledge of ratchets."

"You think that'll work?" Alvin asked doubtfully.

"I can't guarantee you anything," I told him, "but I'll tell you this much. It's going to work better than your other attempt."

I was right that time. Alvin got his job, and he's completely happy doing the work he knows best.

1

OBNOXIOUS POWER

Oliver's Ordeal

We use the term *power* constantly, and yet, while most of us are aware of its meaning, many of us, like Alvin, confuse the trappings of power with the ability to wield power. This ability belongs ultimately to the person who possesses power, to the man or woman with clout.

Webster defines power as "the possession of sway or controlling influence over others." But this is the second definition of power. The dictionary's first definition is "ability, whether physical or moral, to act."

The first definition, *the ability to act,* is really what power is all about. This type of power is creative. It comes from an individual's strength, physical or mental or moral. It was also the kind of power my friend Alvin possessed, but did not completely understand. It was his power to design ratchets, and better ratchets than anyone else. The greater a man's ability, the more creative power he wields.

The other kind of power which concerns itself with influence, control or sway must ultimately become manipulative. It is the power that corrupts men. Baron Acton, who lived in the latter part of the 19th century, wrote, "Power tends to corrupt, and absolute power corrupts absolutely." None of the so-called "power games" are free of this corruption. The manifestation of this type of power inevitably becomes obnoxious and arrogant. The people who use such obnoxious power make us uncomfortable and uneasy. We become aware that we are being manipulated, and we resent the manipulation.

Even when we are not aware of the manipulation on a conscious level, an unconscious part of our minds registers it and resents it.

If the person using this obnoxious power to manipulate us has enough clout, we may be helpless, and usually, the best we can do is bow gracefully to the inevitable, usually—but not always. There are sometimes alternatives, though we may not be aware that they exist.

Oliver Treadwell was trapped in this type of situation. He told me that he worked for a man who used his power in an obnoxious way. One of his favorite ploys was the "blotting out the light" game. It worked this way: when Oliver was on the phone, his boss would walk up to his desk and, as Oliver put it, "blot out the light! He'd just stand there looming over me like some gigantic bird of prey, not saying anything, but looming.

"No matter who I was talking to, no matter what kind of business deal it was, I'd have to mutter, 'Let me call you back.' Hang up and give the boss my full attention."

"And I guess he knew what he was doing," I said.

"Damn right he did! He'd smile like a vulture

and say, 'Don't let me interrupt you, Treadwell,' Christ! When he does it, I begin to stammer and stutter, and I feel like a kid caught with his hand in the cookie jar, like I've done something wrong, like I'm some kind of idiot.''

There were other obnoxious power games that Oliver's boss was fond of playing. ''Nobody's home on the telephone'' was another favorite. He'd call Oliver when he knew he was out to lunch, and he'd leave a message with Oliver's secretary. When Oliver tried to call back, the boss would be ''in conference.''

''In conference! More likely he was in the john—he has a private john in his office, Oliver told me glumly. ''I'd leave word that I'd called and goddamn if he wouldn't call me when I was away from my desk. He must have clocked every move I made. I'd try to return his call, and he'd be 'unavailable right now, Mr. Treadwell. I'll take a message.' That could go on for days, and if I met him in the hall and tried to ask what he wanted, he'd brush past in a big hurry, 'Call me on that, Treadwell.' ''

Oliver sighed. ''It wears me down. I just can't cope with games like that. My work is beginning to suffer and my home life is falling apart.''

Listening to Oliver recite the list of power games his boss played, I finally grew impatient. ''Look,'' I said, ''why do you stand for it?''

He looked at me as if I were crazy. ''I've got to stand for it. He's the boss.''

''You have your options . . .'' I began, but he cut me off.

''What options? I need the job.''

''Then don't complain.''

16

He looked at me with pained eyes. "Hey, you've always been sympathetic. You were the one shoulder I could cry on."

"Cry away, when they're honest tears," I said, "but you have an out. If the boss is that kind of a guy, quit."

"Are you nuts? You can't just walk away from a good-paying job."

"Of course you can. No matter how good the job is, if the working conditions stink you should quit. You're good in your field, good enough to find another job eventually."

He nodded thoughtfully. "But quitting—I'd lose my unemployment insurance, and it would be a rough deal . . ."

"Make the choice. Weigh one against the other, the obnoxious power games of your boss against the difficulty of being temporarily unemployed. Now if you were the kind of man who couldn't find another job, I'd say stick it out. But you could find work. At the worst you'd go through an uncomfortable dry spell. Would a new job be worth it?"

"It damn well would be." He hesitated for a long moment, then said, "You know, you've got something there."

"Okay, and once you've made a firm decision to leave, play the power game yourself."

Startled, he asked, "How would I do that?"

"Try pulling the phone trick on him, looming over his desk, or when he does it, simply put your hand over the mouthpiece and say, 'Would you mind stepping back? This is an important call. I'll be off the phone in a minute.' "

Oliver's eyes gleamed. "I'd like that, but he'd probably fire me."

"All the better. Then you'd collect unemployment insurance. The moment you decide not to take his crap anymore, he'll be powerless to play his games."

Oliver went along with my suggestion, but he gave himself an edge of safety. He told me later that he wasn't the type to risk unemployment. "Maybe I'm too insecure, though my wife agreed with you. Anyway, I found a more comfortable out. I went job hunting first while I was still working for the old game player. I found a good position at almost the same salary. I guess I'm better than I think. I did have options." He smiled. "But before I left, I did play the game you suggested."

"And he fired you?"

Oliver laughed. "Hell no! He must have sensed a new confidence in my attitude. Maybe he realized I didn't care. Anyway, he did an about-face, became more respectful. I suddenly realized he needed me, and if I wanted to I could get some of my own back."

"Did you?"

"No." Oliver shrugged. "I didn't want to play games, and I didn't want to work for a game player, no matter how well he tried to behave himself. I took the other job, and I'm glad I did."

The Power Players

Oliver was fortunate in being able to get out of a game-playing business situation. Many people can't and they have to learn how to cope with the power players, to fight back or to submit gracefully. Unhappily, there are a great many of these rather obnoxious games going on in all walks of business. I learned most of what I know about them from a series of talks with my friend, Nelson Bittersley.

Nelson is an imposing man, over six feet tall, with steady eyes, quiet hands with broad fingers and a solid, comforting presence. Even his name seems to exude power. Nelson is good-looking with a rather large nose that seems to suit his size; indeed, it give him an air of strength.

"An entirely deceptive air," Nelson assured me in his quiet, low-pitched voice. "I am the original sad sack."

"Now, come on," I protested. "Just look at yourself."

"That's just it. Look at me. I radiate confidence and power, and I seem to present a challenge to every man I work with."

"What sort of challenge?"

"I honestly think people get their jollies by screwing me. I've been on the receiving end of more power maneuvers than you can imagine. I'll go out to lunch with some executive in the company, and right away he starts the territory trick."

"Which is?"

"He'll begin to stake out my side of the table. First he'll casually move his cigarettes, his lighter, his eyeglasses, even his butter plate and water glass closer and closer to the center of the table. You know, when two people eat there's an invisible line down the center of the table marking each one's territory. Well, by the end of the first course he's taken over most of my territory and I'm at a disadvantage."

"I can see how that would upset you."

"It does. You know, he's the same kind of guy who comes into my office for a conference and takes over my chair and my desk, who'll use my telephone, even my secretary—again he moves in on my entire territory! It unnerves me."

"But if you know the trick, can't you retaliate, do something about it?"

Nelson looked hurt. "I'm not that kind of person." He shook his head. "The games those players play! There was a guy I used to deal with, a good man, but he had this little trick of coming fifteen minutes late to every appointment. We'd make a date for lunch, and inevitably he'd be there fifteen minutes after the time we agreed on. You could set your watch by it, and even though I knew he'd be late, I'd get annoyed, angry and off balance.

"When he'd finally arrive, full of apologies, I was in no mood to swing any acute business deal. It always gave him an advantage. I came to hate that man, but you know, it's a very common trick, the *last maneuver*. It's first cousin to the *keep 'em waiting trick*, where someone will keep you waiting in his outer office or reception room for a quarter of an hour past the time of your appointment."

"Is it always a quarter of an hour?"

"Sure. That's a good time because it's long enough to get you upset, but not quite long enough to justify your getting up and walking out. To play the game with finesse you have to know your opponent's limitations. Some people have very short fuses and the power player won't ever give them more than ten minutes. Other phlegmatic types can be kept waiting for half an hour. I know one guy who was forgotten in an outer office and simply fell asleep."

20

"Honest?"

"Really. Luckily the cleaning lady woke him up and he was so ashamed he never mentioned it to the guy he was waiting for. You know, a variation of the same game is to be on the telephone when your secretary shows in a client. You wave him to a seat, smile apologetically and keep nodding to the phone for another five minutes. The client gets edgy, and you give the impression that you're really in control of things, especially if you don't talk on the phone, just an occasional 'ahum.' Sounds as if someone is desperately trying to convince you of something and you have enough power to not even answer."

"In fact," I said, "there doesn't have to be anyone else on the phone."

"You've got it. But if you think those games are bad, I had another colleague who uses the *top-you maneuver*. Everything I did, he did one better. I came to work at nine, he'd be there at eight-thirty—or at least he'd tell me he had been. I'd work late at night, and he'd tell me he'd been in all day Saturday. If I came in on Saturday, you could bet your sweet bippy he had been there on Sunday. Anything I did in that firm, he did better, or he let everyone know he did, in no uncertain terms. It gave him an edge on me, a power edge. When promotion time came, salary raises, vacation choices—it was just natural that he should be first in line. I didn't last long with that outfit."

"Was your next job any better?" I asked uneasily.

"Well, there was less one-upmanship, but my associate there was a memo writer. For sheer power plays there's little to top the confirmed memo writer. Ralph used to write a memo on everything that happened, he'd get a phone call, wham!—a memo went out. His books were balanced—a memo. He'd notice that the secretaries left at different times—a memo. The cafeteria served the same meal two days in a row—a memo! I swear, a memo went out every time he went to the bathroom."

"But what good did all those memos do him?"

"There is power in memos. Everyone in the company read them, and gradually Ralph became better known than the boss. It was his way of making himself an important wheel, not just a cog. It didn't matter what the memos said, the fact of their existence was enough."

He continued thoughtfully. "Ralph's memo routine was almost as big a power grabber as another guy I worked with, a *naysayer*."

"What's a naysayer?"

"A man who says nay, or no. He says no to everything, to every proposal, every decision, every choice. He can always be counted on to say no, no matter what the question is."

"I don't see the power there," I frowned.

"Don't you? Well, every firm likes a naysayer. They all want someone who'll say 'no' for the higher-ups. It's a difficult thing to be a consistent doubter, but in a large company it pays off if you can accentuate the negative. The higher-ups can put the naysayer in an important position where everything channels through him. They can always say take it up with *him*, and then they're in the clear. He does their dirty work, and if they want to say yes, over his no, then they become heroes.

"What they don't always realize is that by giving

22

the naysayer the power to turn things down, they're also giving him power, period. There's a lot of power in *no*."

The Gentle Seduction

My friend Nelson is unfortunate in having so many power plays aimed at him, but the use of power in business is familiar to all of us. The men and women who play these games have been fair targets for novels, plays and motion pictures. They are good examples of the corruption of power, though in all fairness, there are many people in power who do not abuse their strength, who treat their subordinates decently and refuse to be drawn into power games.

What differentiates these people who seem able to handle power from those who can't? One possible answer may come out of a still unfinished study being conducted by a team of young sociologists at a major university who asked not to be identified.

"We don't want to release any information until our study is complete," the senior investigator told me. "We've been studying men who, by their associates' reports, are unable to handle power comfortably. We do personality profiles on them and match the results against the profiles of other men who cannot deal with power."

"What have you found?" I asked, but he shook his head.

"It's far too early to give you any firm results, but we do have an indication."

"I'll take that."

"All right. Preliminary research seems to show that people who handle power wisely are more

23

secure in their personality, better able to cope with life in general."

"I think I could have told you that from observation alone," I said.

"Sure you could, but we want scientific validation for it."

If his validation does assure him that secure people are better equipped to handle power, it will not lessen the fact that there is something about power that is irresistible. In one way or another it tends to corrupt even the most secure people, and this is true whether the power is held by a boss, an executive, a foreman, a union official or a shop steward.

The most obvious area where power leads to corruption is politics. Often the corruption sets in before the power is obtained. The struggle to rise in the political world usually strips away a man's morality, layer by layer.

A recent motion picture, *The Seduction of Joe Tynan,* makes a telling point of this theme. A politician, played by Alan Alda, is a thoroughly likeable character throughout the picture, and yet, step by step, he is seduced by the promise of power. He loses his daughter's love in the process and practically destroys his marriage.

We can all understand the pull of political power. We see it on a national as well as international scale. We see revolutions against despots or corrupt men sold out by power-hungry dictators or politicians. We are affected ourselves by the power-plays of the oil-rich countries pitted against the technology-rich ones, and at one time or another each of us has come up against the power of bureaucracy.

But it is harder to understand how power games, so efective in business and politics, can work within the family or among friends. It's hard because, all too often, the trappings of power are different at this level and sometimes the rules of the power game are turned topsy-turvy.

The Gentle Touch

Take Emily and Dave. Emily is a delicate woman, soft-voiced and small, and Dave is an outgoing, boisterous man. They've been married for about thirty years, and on their thirtieth anniversary a group of close friends gave them a big surprise party.

The party lasted well into the morning, and case after case of champagne was put away. Dave, in a delighted state of euphoria, kept telling his friends how wonderful they were, what a great party it was and what a marvelous time he was having.

At two in the morning, thoroughly soaked in champagne, Dave was asked by his best friend, Rick, "Now what present would you like? And don't give me that 'I've got everything routine.' You name it, and I'll see that you get it—anything."

"Hey Rick! After a party like this, what else could a man want?"

"Well, that's what I wanna know," Rick asked drunkenly.

Dave paused, looked around the room at his dearest friends and his wife of thirty years, smiled wistfully and answered, "What I'd really like is a divorce."

There was a moment of shocked silence. Then, treating it as a joke, though in bad taste, the laughter broke out. The party ended soon, but the next day Rick took Dave aside. "You were bombed out of your mind last night. Do you know what you said?" Rick was a bit angry about it all. He was very fond of Emily.

Looking at him thoughtfully, Dave said, "Sure I know. After thirty years I want out. I want a divorce."

"But why? Emily is—hell, she's the gentlest, sweetest person in our crowd. If she were like my wife . . ." Rick rolled his eyes. "That one's a ball-breaker. Mind you, I can handle her, but she fights me every inch of the way."

"But who wears the pants in your family?" Dave asked.

"Why, I do. She may rant and rave, but I stick to my guns. After all, I make the dough—I say how we spend it. Anyway, we both enjoy the fighting—but your Emily . . ."

"Have you any idea, Rick," Dave asked slowly, "of the power a woman like Emily can wield? Have you any idea of the guilt a man can build up during thirty years of marriage to someone like that? In thirty years I've never dared to insist on what I want. Oh, not that Emily would oppose me. Heaven forbid. She'd just let me know what she wanted and give me that tremulous smile, and I'd feel like a louse."

"Oh, come on, you've got to be kidding!"

"Kidding? I'm dead serious. You can't fight someone like that. I've given in on every issue we have ever had. It's always, 'We'll do what you like, Dave.' But we never do. She lets me know what she wants with a sigh, and by God, we do it! I'd feel like a complete shit if we didn't."

"You know, I made that remark about wanting a divorce when I was drunk. Sure, I want it, but I'll never have the guts to go for it. Just like you say, how could I do that to a sweet, gentle woman like Emily?

"And if I try to oppose her, I get those tears welling up in her soft doe-like eyes. There's a lot of power in a woman's tears, especially when every other man in our crowd admires Emily. The perfect doormat of a wife—if they only knew!"

Dave's dilemma isn't surprising. What is surprising is that so few of us see through the trappings of power in this type of relationship. Here, paradoxically, the strength belongs to the weak.

What are the elements that go into this power play?

Emily is involved in a game as old as mankind—the *martyr syndrome*. Mel Brooks, in his very funny routine about the 2000-year-old man, tells of a caveman's parents coming to visit and insisting, while standing out in the rain, that they were all right. "Enjoy yourself, don't bother about us."

This is the classic martyr's ploy. First put yourself at a disadvantage, then insist that it's all right. "I'm really not important enough for you to fuss over," is what you appear to say. What's implied, however is, "You're not decent enough to insist on fussing over me. Ignore me, as I urge you to, and it proves you're selfish."

When the person playing the martyr is bound to you by legal or family ties—a father, a mother, a wife, a husband—there is enormous power in his position. Our culture demands that you honor your father and mother, care for your children and "cleave unto" your spouse till death do you part.

With these principles drummed into you, you are fair game for the guilt aroused by the *martyr syndrome*. Will you admit to yourself that you're a selfish stinker? How many of us can find the strength to do it, or to ignore the martyr's unspoken demands and realize that we are not at fault?

Dave couldn't even though the demands were so gentle, so sensitive—or perhaps for that very reason. In the beginning of his marriage he reacted automatically to Emily's sweet compliance without realizing that he was giving in. He assumed he was the strong one in the relationship, the boss in his own home. He was certainly stronger physically. His wife seemed ready to submit to his every wish—at least she said she did. It was just fortunate that his wishes seemed to coincide with hers—or if they didn't, it was no effort to change his. She was so sweet about it, why deny her what little she asked for? But small demands, prettily put, grow bigger and more frequent with time, and in thirty years sweetness cloys. Somewhere, well along in their marriage, Dave became aware of where the power really lay. But by then it was too late to do anything about it—or so he felt. He was trapped into a low-power role with a high-power appearance.

It is unlikely that someone like Dave will ever break out of his role. A thirty-year habit it too hard to overcome, and most of us would shake our heads and say, "What is Dave getting out of this relationship? There must be some goodies in giving in on every issue. In some way this must feed his ego and give him enough satisfaction to stay on in the relationship."

For any martyr role to work over an extended period of time, the martyr's partner must get something, if not in real benefits, then in imagined ones. It may be no more than his conviction that he is a hero for giving in, and his heroism may be enough reward in itself.

If he knows he is not a hero, then his friends, neighbors and family may consider him one, and their praise may be reward enough. Look what he puts up with! Only a saint would stand for that! The sacrifices he's made!

When such praise is the reward, the hero has become something of a martyr himself, and the roles are confused. When the hero serving a martyr becomes a martyr too, you can be sure that a struggle for power is going on—an obnoxious struggle for an obnoxious sort of power.

Martyr Power

The power Emily wielded over Dave is common in a marriage, but as a psychologist friend pointed out to me, "The real power in marriage usually resides with the one who controls the financial dispensations."

"You mean the breadwinner?"

"Exactly." Frowning a bit, he went on slowly. "We live in a male-dominated, male-oriented society, and, as a rule, it follows that the power is in the male's hands. It is men who lay down the rules, men who make our laws and run the country, and their strength, their power, flows from the fact that they are the money-makers."

Listening to him, I thought of Rick's answer to Dave's question about who wore the pants in their family. "But isn't all this changing with woman's lib?" I asked.

"To a small degree. A greater change has come because of inflation and the need for women as well as men to work and bring home a wage. More and more, the only way a family can survive is by the woman joining the man in the breadwinning role. You see, the one who makes the money is the one who usually holds the power. When both work, the woman almost always make less than the man, and he still has an edge on power."

"But when the woman does make more money?"

"Ah, then you often get marital problems. Sometimes the marriage can't take the strain, and it ends in divorce. What usually happens is that the man can't accept the subordinate position that goes with bringing home a smaller paycheck. An interesting fact came out of all that fuss about ERA, the Equal Rights Amendment. One of the big fears men had was that women would make more money if given equal opportunity, and the society would end up with men being subservient."

"But the power isn't always with the breadwinner," I pointed out, and I told him the story of Dave and Emily. "Sometimes you may have a stronger power base because of your weakness."

Nodding, he said, "Yes, and traditionally women have been driven into that role, whether it's the delicate martyr like your Emily, or the tough, long-suffering mother-martyr. I had a patient whose mother ruled the family with an iron hand. She was always ill, and she used her illness to get whatever she wanted. Not like Emily, but very openly. She operated from a position of power, of martyr power, but there was nothing delicate or gentle about her. She constantly told her children about the sacrifices she had made for them, the things she had given up, the suffering they had caused her.

"Two of her three boys were overwhelmed with guilt and spent their lives trying to pacify her, to make up for all her sacrifices."

"And the third?"

"He left home at sixteen, ran off and never returned. I don't know what kind of a life he had, but I suspect he was a survivor. The only way he could handle her power play was to turn his back on her. My patient, the oldest son, was unable to make a life of his own. He saw marriage as a betrayal of his mother. How could he leave her for another woman when she needed him so? That was a classic case of blatant martyr power."

"But doesn't that disprove your statement about the men holding the power?"

"No. No more than it disproves the fact that many men, in a family setting, resort to the martyr ploy themselves to gain power. Mothers get the bad press, but there are many fathers who constantly remind their children and wives of the sacrifices they have made for them.

"Basically, martyrdom is the use of guilt to keep power concentrated in your own hands. I've seen it operate on all levels. Parents will make their children feel guilty in order to keep the upper hand, but children will also make their parents feel guilty for the same reason. I've seen children of five and six and even younger latch onto the power-through-guilt routine and manipulate their parents to get what they want."

"Does it happen in business, too?" I asked.

"Very often. A secretary will do it to her boss. It's not common among assembly line workers, because to be effective it needs a one-to-one relationship. A good secretary-boss relationship is like a good marriage. The two work together well. They complement each other and gain benefits from each other. The boss is relieved of onerous duties, and the secretary receives a good salary and prestige. When neither the salary nor the prestige satisfy the secretary's inner needs, she may begin to lay a guilt trip on her boss in order to gain martyr power, or he may play the martyr in order to tighten his control over her.

"The same game can be played between bosses and executives, but it works best in a male-female situation, even when there is no open sex relationship."

"Why do you say open?"

"Because every male-female relationship has sexual overtones, boss-secretary, social friends, even father-daughter—especially father-daughter!" He laughed. "But you don't want to get into Freud right now, do you?"

I assured him I didn't, but the sexual aspect of power games is an intriguing one. Take the story of Norman and Addie.

They were very much in love, and while their backgrounds were different, their goals were very similar. Addie worked in an office by day as a typist and wrote at night. She had published a few articles and was sure she would some day make it as a full-time writer.

"My daytime job is to feed, shelter and clothe me," she told Norman. "All I live for is the day I can give it up."

Norman waited tables in a small restaurant at night and painted during the day. He understood Addie's longing. "Painting is what I live for. Waiting tables makes it possible for me to paint—why don't we pool our resources and move in together?"

They had been lovers for four months, but Addie was doubtful. "Living with someone's a very heavy trip, Norman. I don't really know where you're coming from. I couldn't take that *macho* scene."

"You know me better than that," Norman was offended. "We share and share alike, but we each do our thing. The point is, we'll have each other full time. How about that?"

Addie wasn't absolutely sure about this living arrangement, but she was pretty sure that she loved Norman. Finally she gave in. She did, however, insist that they write out a "contract of cohabitation" splitting the work right down the middle.

Norman was delighted. "This way we each have our own responsibility. Great!" In fact, he had the contract framed and hung up on the kitchen wall.

"That way it'll always be there to remind us."

The apartment they found had two bedrooms, and they each took one as a studio and turned the living room into a shared bedroom. They posted rosters of laundry, cleaning, cooking, shopping and all the other duties, share-and-share-alike, as Norman insisted.

It was a lovely set-up. The nicest part of all, Norman insisted, cuddling up with Addie in bed one night, "is that I don't have to get up and go home now—I am home!"

"Your feet are cold." Addie sat up in bed. "I just can't sleep. I'm going to make a pot of tea."

When Norman came into the kitchen a half hour later, yawning and tying his bathrobe, he found Addie at the kitchen sink, her arms in soapy water.

"What on earth are you doing?"

"I'm re-doing. You had pots and pans tonight, and as usual they're full of grease."

"Hey, I'm sorry, but you don't have to do it now, at this hour."

"I couldn't even boil water in the kettle it was so yucky."

Norman apologized profusely and Addie made tea for both of them and tried to forget it. What the hell, anyone could fall from grace once. But after the fourth time she found the pots in a mess, she decided pots just weren't Norman's thing. There had to be some reprogramming. "Let's face it, you do a lousy job on pots and pans."

"I'm sorry," Norman said meekly. "I never liked doing dishes."

"Well, neither do I, but we're going to get ptomaine poisoning if you keep on. I'll take this over and you can do the vacuuming from now on."

It was, as Addie realized later, the beginning of trouble in paradise. Norman was perfectly willing to take over any job, the only problem was that he klutzed-out on everything. He washed the colored clothes with the white and turned all Addie's white T-shirts a pale pink. He put the wrong setting on the metered dryer and Addie lost two inches on all her slacks. It was easier for Addie to take over the wash from then on. Norman was crushed. He apologized so abjectly that she hadn't the heart to complain, or point out that the roster was growing lopsided, nor did she complain much when he loused up the shopping and sent their food bills skyrocketing. "We just bought a load of fruit two days ago. What were you thinking of? We can't eat all those peaches in a month! And they're too ripe to keep."

"But they looked so good, and did you ever see plums so juicy? I couldn't resist them." He gave her that little-boy smile. "I guess I loused up again?"

"Oh, it's all right. I'll cook them and freeze them, but next time let me do the shopping."

It happened gradually, but by the end of six months Addie found herself running the house. "It's just more efficient," she shrugged when her friend asked her what had happened to her cohabitation contract. "Oh, that's still up on the kitchen wall, neatly framed—but I get the feeling that I've been framed just as neatly. We share the rent, but that's about all we share now, and Norman's happy as a bedbug. I'm like any married woman with a job. I come home from work and Norman's out waiting tables and the house is a mess. He doesn't seem to notice, so either we live

35

like that, or I clean it, and one by one I've taken on all the jobs. Oh, Norman's sweet about it and calls himself all sorts of names for not doing things right and praises me for my organization and ability—but it all boils down to my doing all the work!"

Addie stuck it out for a year, but when their lease was up she announced firmly that she was going back to single living. "But I love you!" Norman protested. "I thought—well, I thought this would all lead to marraige. I—I feel used!"

"Marriage? No way," Addie said firmly. "I've gotten a taste of real male helplessness, and you can keep it. Lovers, yes. Husband and wife, never!"

"The bottom line," she told her girl friend as she helped Addie unpack boxes in her new apartment, "is who's got the power. Now I'm capable and efficient. Norman's a dreamer and sort of spacy. I love him for those qualities. You can see them in his paintings, but living with him is sheer hell. You see, you just can't fight a weak opponent. He's too powerful! Sounds crazy, and maybe it is, but believe me, for living together, get a strong man. He may be *macho*, but at least he'll take over and do his share—or if he doesn't you can fight like hell."

The power of helplessness is different from the power of a martyr. The martyr arouses guilt. The helpless person can arouse a variety of feelings—pity, solicitude, tenderness, even love—but eventually every one of these emotions will be tinged with resentment. It becomes obvious that helplessness, consciously or unconsciously, is a successful power ploy.

Unfortunately for the winner in the *helplessness game,* victory usually brings rejection as well. The only one who can play to a standstill against a helpless player is a born martyr. When the two get together, you will see a deadly struggle for power that can, if both are evenly matched, lead to a wretched draw.

The Potency of Impotence

There are any number of sexual power games, and most of us play them unconsciously, unaware of what we are doing. I was made aware of this some time ago when I interviewed Dr. William H. Masters and Virginia E. Johnson on their treatment of sexual problems. I was intrigued by the fact that they claimed a high percentage of cures in cases of impotence, premature ejaculation and even frigidity, problems that most therapists found almost incurable.

To get an objective viewpoint of their work, I spoke to a close friend, a psychiatrist who treats sexual problems. "Do you feel their treatment is valid?" I asked her.

She shrugged. "I can only comment on their published results, but one thing makes me uneasy about any attempt to cure sexual problems."

"What is that?" I asked.

"The fact that so many of these so-called problems are really tied up with a struggle for power."

I didn't understand, and she went on to explain. "As an example, I have a patient who came to me with a complaint of premature ejaculation. I should say his wife insisted on treatment. They had been

37

married for ten years, and the problem had grown worse over the years.

"Now the curious thing about it, I found, was that as far as he was concerned, it wasn't a problem at all. It was only his wife who felt that it was destroying their marriage. He seemed quite—well, adjusted is the only word that comes to me. He was adjusted to the situation and had no anxiety about it."

"How curious. I should think he'd be very concerned."

"Yes, wouldn't you? But as I got to understand the situation, I found that I was in the middle of a power struggle. His wife was a very aggressive, very dominating woman who ran his life, controlled the purse strings, dictated what they would do and who they would see. In short, she was a petty tyrant."

"And he stood for it?"

My friend smiled. "We don't all have a choice in these situations. It's not all that simple. He had a mother much like his wife, and both treated him with contempt—but that's only part of the story. What I came to realize was that the only way he could strike back, the only way he could gain power, was sexually."

"I don't understand that. What power did he have if he was a premature ejaculator?"

"But that's just where his power lay. He could deny his wife any satisfaction on this one level. Here was the only situation where he had complete power, and by God he wasn't about to give it up. Nothing I could do would help, and I'm firmly convinced that no technique of Masters and Johnson would help either, not while he remained in that marital situation."

There are other sexual power struggles I learned from my friend. Impotence in a man can be due to a number of physical factors, or, more commonly to psychological factors. One psychological cause is the desire to gain power over a woman. How easy to punish someone by denying them sexual satisfaction, and for this, impotence can be as effective as premature ejaculation. It can also say, "You don't excite me sexually," a perfect sexual put-down.

And this is not ony the man's province, my friend explained. Women too play the sexual power game. Frigidity, the inability to reach orgasm, is almost always psychological, and occasionally it becomes a woman's weapon to use against a man. This works best when it's a selective kind of frigidity. "I don't know what's wrong. I never had this trouble with other men," is a good example of a power put-down.

Here, the power play is doubled. Not only is the man incapable of bringing her to orgasm, but the fault is definitely his, not hers. After all, other men had had no problems. It's a rare man who will ask for references. However he may bluster, he's usually crushed in such a situation and match point goes to the woman.

Those Dirty Little Games

In my pursuit of the truth about the sexual power game, I decided to speak to a real professional, Marlene, a woman who understands all the little tricks of sex. I had first met Marlene on a flight from Los Angeles to New York. She was a tall, stunning blond with pale blue eyes that could warm

you or freeze you with a glance. We were seated together, and we both had a few drinks. During the flight, we came to be good friends. She asked me what I did for a living, and I told her I was a writer.
"And what do you do?"

With the faintest of German accents, Marlene said, "Will it shock you if I confess that I'm a call girl?"

"Surprise me, yes. Shock me, no," I answered, and we had a long, fascinating talk about her profession. She had often thought of writing a book about her experiences. "But the truth is," she sighed, "I'm just too lazy."

At the end of the trip we traded addresses and promised to keep in touch. That had been a year ago, and yet Marlene seemed delighted when I called. "I'd like to talk to you about a book I'm writing. Can we get together?"

"You can take me out to lunch," she said, and I agreed. Over a hearty steak and beer, I asked her about the use of power in her sexual encounters.

"It's a funny thing," she said thoughtfully, "how very few men want to dominate me, to be the aggressor, to show their power. Oh, there are some, yes, but with them I have the feeling that it's pretense."

"What do you mean?"

"I mean they are putting on a show, trying to convince me that they are—how do you say it— *macho*. No, I have found from my long experience—and it has been long, I don't really show my age—I have found that most men want me to dominate them. They love those dirty little games in which I play a part, a—oh, severe schoolmistress, a harsh nun, an angry wife, a strict mother—nowadays even a woman army officer—we go through all the silly routines, the boots and the whip—Ach! Sometimes it turns my stomach." She attacked her steak furiously for a few minutes, then wiped her lips and looked up at me. "Do you know what I'd like? Someday I'd like to meet a real man. I don't even care if he roughed me up, as long as he didn't play games!"

"You mean you'd like someone to dominate you?"

"Well, what's so surprising about that? Believe me, every woman does in her secret fantasies. For political reasons most women won't admit it today, but deep down, in their dreams even, they want it."

There seemed a flaw here that I didn't want to go into with Marlene. If most men wanted to be dominated, and most women do, too—who is going to do the dominating? Who gets to wield the power?

I took the question up with a psychoanalyst, a young man, progressive and eclectic in his approach.

"Of course it's a simplification," he laughed. "Your call-girl friend, for all her experience, meets only a certain type of man, a man who is limited emotionally. He goes to her simply because he cannot conduct a normal relationship. He pays for sex, and because he pays he can be assured of what he wants. The average well-adjusted man has to fight competition in the sexual arena. Inevitably, you're going to find an abnormally high percentage of emotionally crippled men among your call girl's clients."

"It seems to me that you're saying two things.

One, the men who patronize call girls are emotionally crippled."

"Usually, yes."

"And two, that men who want to dominate sexually are also emotionally crippled."

He thought about that very carefully for a while, nodding slowly. "Yes," he said finally, "and I'd go a bit further. The need to be dominated is a kind of mental sickness—but so is the need to dominate. The need to gain power and to use it to subordinate others is also a kind of sickness."

"But isn't it a very human sickness?"

He smiled rather sadly. "Yes, and so is murder and armed robbery, and, of course, war and exploitation—they are all very human even though they are symptoms of the abuse of power."

2

FINDING YOUR POWER PROFILE

The Unhappy Chairman

Through high school and college, Mike Slade and
Paul Golding were close friends. When they were
accepted at the same college, they decided to room
together, and their friendship persisted into
graduate school in spite of their different
temperments—or perhaps because of them. Paul, a
quiet, introspective man, took his masters degree in
medieval studies, while Mike, outgoing and
energetic, chose economics as his field.

"I was really torn," he told Paul. "You know, I
always wanted to go to law school and eventually
get into politics, but the tuition—well, maybe
some day . . ."

After graduate school, Paul considered teaching.
"It's what I really enjoy," he told Mike. "I get
feedback from the kids that blows my mind."

Mike shook his head. "Well, you're good at it. I
watched you in that English course. But you know,
teaching with only a masters is a dead end. You'll
be stuck on a high school level. If we ever want to
get ahead we have to get into a big university and
we need our doctorates for that. What do you
say?"

At first Paul resisted. The few classes he had taught had been exciting, and he couldn't see the need for further education, but eventually Mike convinced him. They applied and were accepted at the same university, and they were both married before they finished their programs. Afterwards, to their delight, they both received professorships at a large, midwestern university.

Over the years their friendship deepened. Paul's marriage broke up, but Mike and his wife saw him through those tough times, and eventually introduced him to the woman who became his second wife. In the meantime they struggled to the tops of their departments. Paul in English and Mike in Economics.

"I guess you've given up on politics," Paul asked Mike one evening over drinks.

"Hell, yes. I haven't got the charisma for it, and anyway, what appealed to me about politics was the power you get when you're successful."

Paul stirred his drink. "There's plenty of power available around here—and all the miserable infighting that goes with it."

"Don't I know it. But, hey, it's not so bad. You know, Paul, I love a good fight. And, I'll tell you something, I've got bigger fish to fry. The Economics Department is kid stuff—boring."

"You're not leaving?" Paul was startled.

Mike laughed. "No way. What this boy is after is a job in administration. That's where the power is. I've been talking to the right guys at the right time, mending a few fences, laying on a little charm. The grapevine tells me that they may hire the new chancellor from the ranks."

"And you're going to take a crack at it?" Paul

raised his glass with a slightly mocking gesture. "Good luck if you can make it—and take it!"

Mike did get the job within a year, with all the power that went along with it, and he felt that he had truly arrived. The only fly in his ointment was Paul's unexpected decision to give up the chairmanship of the English Department.

"But why, Paul, for Christ's sake, now that I'm in a position to really do some good for you. You've been talking about a Drama Department, and I just know I could swing a grant to renovate that old theatre in town. I've got the grants department in my pocket."

"Mike, look—" Paul's voice was tense. "You love all that wheeling and dealing, the cut-throat hassling in this academic set-up. You thrive on it, and maybe it's right for you, but I hate it. It's destroying me!"

"I'm not all that crazy about it," Mike said slowly. "But it's a necessary means to an end. It's where it all gets me that counts." He hesitated. "For me, the important thing is being on top of the heap. It's always been that way."

"But that's just it, Mike. It's not like that for me. So now I'm chairman of my department, but I'm uncomfortable in the job. I'm not a fighter, Mike, and I hate the kind of power I have to use in order to stay chairman. Last week I found myself getting ready to deny one of my associates a grant simply because he was a threat to my position. I can't live with that kind of maneuvering. To tell you the truth, I want to go back to teaching, plain and simple. Okay?"

There was a long silence, then Mike shrugged. "Okay, buddy. We'll drink to my climb up the

45

ivied walls of academe."

"And to my fall!" Paul grinned. "Bottoms up."

Power Profiles

It had taken Paul the better part of his lifetime to recognize a few basic facts about himself. He was not cut out to be a leader, and the use of power made him unhappy. Most important of all, there was no reason why he had to fight his way to the top and then keep fighting to stay there. True, he had the ability to be a leader, and he had the intelligence—he had managed to use both to get to be chairman of his department. But, as he finally realized, he had done it all under the influence of Mike. During those years of struggle he had never questioned whether his friend's standards were right or wrong for him.

"I was never cut out to be anything more than a teacher," he told Mike. "And I'm a damned good one, too. When I taught I felt I was doing something important, even something creative. That's right, there is a creative element in teaching. I was never happy once I got beyond that point." He hesitated. "It's funny, but now I think that was one of the things that destroyed my first marriage."

Later, Mike told his wife, "I don't understand Paul. My God, I love that guy—we grew up together, but I can't figure out why a man doesn't want to do his best. Paul is smart and he can handle authority. He proved that while he was chairman of the English Department. He did a damned fine job."

"What you don't understand," his wife told him gently, "is that Paul does his best when he's teaching. Teaching is his best—nothing more, nothing less. Now your best is running things, being the big boss, and you have the energy for it, the drive, too. Paul is sort of—well, lower-keyed, gentler."

Instinctively, Mike's wife knew that Mike needed power. He thrived on it, and he was able to handle it. He had a *strong power profile*. A man's power profile is the overall view of his personality. It shows his strengths and weaknesses, his tenacity and moral fibre, his ability to lead or to follow, his tendency to be outgoing or introverted, his creative ability or lack of it, as well as a dozen other traits. When an analysis of all these attributes is drawn up, one can determine whether a person is oriented towards power, as Mike was, or away from it, as Paul was.

However, in spite of his low power profile, Paul was able to reach a position of power and hold it competently for a while. He could learn to take and use power because he was an intelligent man, but he was never able to be happy with power. Nor did he ever want it. He took it because he had grown up strongly influenced by the same philosophy that had influenced Mike. *Grab power when you can. We must all exert ourselves to the limits of our potential. A man's reach should exceed his grasp.*

The mottoes were all well and good for Mike. Indeed, he thrived on them, but they were all wrong for Paul. The power he wielded succeeded only in depressing him. He was a man who should never had tried for power. If, in some way, he had come to understand this earlier in his life, he would have

47

been much happier.

The Corruption of Power

At this point it's well to stress the fact that there is nothing wrong with wanting power, if you genuinely want it. In the same way there is nothing right about such wants. They are simply a normal fact of life for people with strong power profiles. But there are power pitfalls. If you want power and you need it, how will you go about getting it?

The first chapter detailed some of the unhappy results of the wrong way of getting power as well as the misuse of power. The corruption that goes with power is also a very real danger, and there are many ways in which it can work.

People like Mike who are power-positive develop a style of life and action that draws attention to themselves. People admire them and follow them—which is one of the big attractions of power. The admiration and esteem of others is the greatest reason for wanting and gaining power. Along with the power goes social influence and a position of authority. People come to respect the powerful man and do as he suggests, even when they don't have to.

This is the point of temptation. How easy to misuse power. How simple to justify the misuse. But once the line is crossed, the people who have followed the leader, respected him and looked up to him, will begin to have second thoughts. Perhaps he isn't quite the ideal leader they expected. In fact, his feet may actually be made of clay!

The man of power can have two reactions to this situation. If he is very wise, he will draw back and reconsider his own actions. He may ask himself, "Have I been following the right track? Have I been handling my department with consideration and fairness? Do my orders always make sense, or are they just ways of demonstrating my authority?" If he can answer these questions honestly, he may then set out to correct his mistakes and win back the respect of his followers.

But what if he is less than wise? What if the taste of power has spoiled his judgment, or if he panics at the thought of losing any of it? Then he may respond to criticism by tightening the reins, by using even greater dictatorial methods to keep everyone under him in line. He has taken the first step towards becoming a petty tyrant, and he may even think seriously about the next step—manipulating any information about the mistakes he has made.

Dictators, army strong-men, bureaucrats, union officials, corporate executives, presidents of countries, mayors, governors, and senators have all gone this route in order to keep their power, or to give the impression that their power still comes through the will of those under them.

Eventually, the corrupting power may lead a man inward. If the real world deprives him of his power, he may construct a fantasy world and isolate himself from reality, create his own easily-controlled universe where he can continue to be superior. If he has the financial power, he may end up as a walled-off, protected recluse, or, lacking the money, he may retreat all the way into a neurotic or psychotic state, into insanity or near insanity.

49

Howard Hughes was a classic example of this. And movie stars, unable to handle the power of fame, sometimes have also chosen this route of isolation.

As dreadful as these results of the corruption of power may be, it is still obvious that at this point in civilization there must be men who can hold power and use it. There must be leaders, and there must be followers. Each of us, if we ever face the possibility of attaining significant power, must ask ourselves, is it right for me to gain power and to use it, or is it wrong? Is it right for me to claw my way up the business ladder through the obnoxious use of power, as so many current books advise, or is this an emotional dead end? Will it turn me into a detestable human being? And if it does, do I really care, or is the power I gain reward enough? And, of course, the ultimate question—can I get and hold power and still remain a decent human being?

Inevitably, the answers must depend on the type of person you are. We must turn the questions around. Instead of asking, "Should I live with power?" you must ask, "*Can* I do so?" Instead of, "How can I get to the top?" ask, "Am I the sort of man who *should* attempt the climb?" And then, the key question becomes not, "How will I handle power?" as much as, "Can I *bear* to handle it?"

In the final analysis, the question of whether to go for power is a deeply personal one and it must be answered from your individual power motivation, your individual power profile.

Interior vs. Exterior

There are guidelines that could have helped Paul determine his power profile earlier, guidelines that can help any of us discover what direction we should take in terms of power. Or whether we should be content to be a follower, strive to become a leader or try to stay independent, neutral. There are also guidelines that can help us discover our own potential and develop it to its fullest.

People like Paul, who are uncomfortable with power, tend to be *interior* people. They are usually creative, no matter what their field, and they are often self-sufficient, able to spend time with themselves.

Exterior people are more practical. They are most comfortable with other people, and they like to manage other people. They tend to organize their own lives better. They can also handle power well and are most comfortable with it.

Exterior people are more likely to desire power, so the first step is to discover whether you are an interior person or an exterior one. Many of us know exactly what we are, but most of us don't. We have fanciful ideas about our own personality. Confronted with a truth about our actions, we often seem surprised or bewildered. "I'm not like that at all. Actually, I'm very easygoing," or "I'm very assertive," or "Me stubborn? Not a bit!"

To wipe away some of these self-delusions, try answering the following set of questions. When you have finished you will have some insight into your own personality, whether you are an interior person or an exterior one.

A number of situations are presented and after each there are three alternative methods of behavior. Choose the method that is closest to the way you would act. In reading the situation through, try to put yourself into the action. Think of the other characters as friends you know, actual people.

The Apartment

You have decided to move and have been shown a number of apartments. Now you walk into the latest with the renting agent and find that it is a large, roomy place with high ceilings, a working fireplace and a beautiful view from the living room windows. It had a northern exposure and the windows don't work too well. In fact, neither does the plumbing, and the kitchen, for all its spaciousness, is poorly laid out and inefficient. The carpeting will have to be replaced and the floors underneath it look shabby. On the other hand, the rent is low and the neighborhood is a very good one. What do you do?

(A) You take the apartment without much hesitation. After all, the view alone is worth it, and those high ceilings give an air of grandeur to the rooms. The real clincher, however, is the fireplace. How wonderful on a cold winter night!

(B) Sure, the view and the fireplace and the ceilings are great, but let's think about the exposure and the plumbing and that kitchen. What's it going to take to get it into working order? Or, for that matter, the carpeting has to come up and won't the floors need redoing? Let's consider all the pros and cons before we rush into it.

(C) It's a good buy in terms of what has to be done balanced against the low rent. I'll take it because it's in a very good neighborhood and that's going to impress people. It's good for my image. Once I get it into shape, it's the kind of place that will have a pretty classy look.

The Vacation

You and your wife have finally gotten enough scratch together to go off on that long-anticipated vacation. The only problem is where to go. You consult your travel agent and get a long list of all the possible places and prices, but still, you have trouble deciding.

(A) You decide on the Club Internationale and their trip to Marakesh and some nearby exotic islands. True, most of the club members do not speak English, and it is very "pricey," but there is such a romantic sound to Marakesh and those far-off places.

(B) You settle for an island in the West Indies. It's very accessible and the price is right. Besides, it has marvelous beaches and few people.

(C) It costs more than you figured on paying, but you make reservations at the famous White Springs Hotel. Everything is available there, and it's a practical place to rest or play. Besides, it's the "in" place this year and you know some very important people who'll be there.

The Passing Years

The situation is universal. Combing your hair that morning, you suddenly notice that there is more grey then color. Somehow, almost overnight it seems, the years have caught up with you. A closer look in the mirror shows you that indeed there are new lines at the corners of your eyes and a scattering of wrinkles. Where did those come from? No doubt about it. You are getting old.

(A) This becomes one of the worst days of your life. There seem to be more young and beautiful people around then ever before. When the chips are down you'd give just about anything for your lost youth!

(B) Well, there you are. It was bound to happen sooner or later, but it's not the end of the world. There are things you can do about aging, even if it's only touching up your hair. Let's check them out.

(C) How about that! You've finally gotten that distinguished touch of grey. Character lines and all. It was bound to happen. What the hell!

Love and Marriage

Well, it's that time of your life. You've got a good job and there's finally some direction to your life. You're sick of the singles scene and you want to settle down. What kind of a partner are you going to look for?

(A) Whoever you spend the rest of your life with has got to be the best. You begin to look for someone beautiful or handsome, talented or brilliant, a well-rounded person with excellent taste and a fine background, but above all someone who will turn you on—and on!

(B) Good-looking? Sure, and at least as smart as I am, but above all, you search for someone you can get along with.

(C) Looks? Character? Okay, but first and foremost you want someone who can help you out, who can be an asset. A private income or good earning power doesn't hurt either. It's as easy to fall in love with a rich person as with a poor one. But someone you'll be proud to walk down the street with, someone with class, someone everyone else can envy.

And Now the Kids

You and your wife or husband are just about into your thirties and you've been to visit your closest friend and her new baby. The baby is an absolute miracle, and you come home very thoughtful. That night you decide you both must talk about passing on your own wonderful genes.

(A) You are absolutely certain that you must have a houseful of darling children, or at least five. Or, you are very firm about zero population growth and you seriously think you'll have no children at all.

(B) Undoubtedly babies are major miracles, and why not start planning for them now—at least two—spaced about two years apart.

(C) Yes, your friend's baby was a doll, but let's not rush into anything just yet. Let's consider our income and how important babies are to someone in my position.

What Kind of a Person Am I?

It should become obvious, as you read through the different problems, that for every situation presented there are the same three types of behavior. (A) is the approach that the interior type of person is most likely to take. If you have chosen it in most situations, then your own emotional reactions are most important to you. Power is something you can easily do without. If most of your choices have been (C), then you are an exterior person. You are very practical, calculating and well organized. It's likely that you enjoy power and can handle it.

If, like the great majority of people, you fall into the (B) pattern, then you can react as an interior person or an exterior one depending on the situation. If power comes your way, you can probably handle it, but the chances are you won't go looking for it.

The Dominance Quotient

Discovering whether your personality is interior, exterior or a little of both is the first step towards exploring your ability to handle power and discovering your power profile. While it is true that the great majority of power-hungry people are exterior people, it doesn't follow that all exterior people are eager for power, nor that most interior people are indifferent to it. There are other personality traits that must be considered, and one of the most important of these is dominance.

Each of us has what might be called a

Dominance Quotient, or DQ, a measurable amount of a trait that can best be expressed as a need to dominate others. To see your power profile from a different angle, you must consider next just how high your DQ is. Are you happiest dominating others, or does being dominated by someone else turn you on? This is an area where it is very difficult to be most honest about yourself. Dominance, along with aggression, has been labeled unpleasant in our culture, and indeed it often is. But many times it is also a necessary quality.

How dominant are you? What do you really know about your need to dominate others? Many dominating people are genuinely shocked when they hear of their own actions. "Me? But I'm so easily swayed!" While other, easily manipulated people, see themselves as extremely dominant. "I don't take crap from anyone. I'm my own man."

The best way to discover some of the truth about yourself and dominance is to answer very honestly the following set of questions. Obviously, the person who wants to dominate the situation is the same person who wants power. The person who doesn't care about dominance is usually the one who doesn't hanker after power.

Again, there are different situations with three different types of reaction for each. Read the situation and imaginatively place yourself in it, then chose the course of action you would be most likely to follow.

The Conversation

It's after dinner and you're all sitting around the

living room, a group of pleasant, friendly people. The talk drifts along aimlessly, but trenchantly, covering a number of very fascinating subjects. You're all relaxed and comfortable.

(A) You listen more often then you talk, and you are sure you are getting a great deal out of this evening. A lot of heavy stuff you were uncertain about seems to be clearer. You are really enjoying yourself.

(B) You listen to what the others have to say, but you don't hesitate to put your own views forward. You certainly give as much as you get, and you come away feeling you've learned a lot. You've opened a few other minds to the truth.

(C) You talk much more than you listen because you have some very important things to say about all these matters, and you know the rest will want to hear your ideas. In fact, you often have to interrupt some irrelevant talk to get your own point across, but then it's worth it.

Chow Time

The movie was great and now the six of you are standing on a street corner trying to decide where to go for a good meal. This is your home town, but it's a big place and you don't know all of it.

(A) You listen to all the recommendations, hoping that they will come up with a good suggestion and you'll find a great new restaurant to eat in.

(B) You listen to all the other suggestions, including the one from the nut who wants to drive 12 miles to a truck stop diner. Then you put your own two cents in—you opt for that little Italian place

58

that makes their own pasta. In the end, however, you go along with the majority, or the one that sounds best.

(C) Never mind those places—you know this terrific charcoal broil spot where they let you brand your own steaks, and the vegetables are out of this world. You insist everyone go there because you know they'll love it.

On the Job

Things haven't been going well in your department, through no one's fault, and now one of the executives has come up with a far-out idea that could really save the day—if it works. From your point of view it looks very good, very good indeed!

(A) It looks good on paper, but if you try it out and it fails you'll all be up the creek with no paddle. Why take the chance? Or if anyone goes out on the limb, let it be the guy who thought up the plan.

(B) It seems like a sound plan, and you're pretty sure it will work even though it's far out. Still, why should you be the fall guy? Let's put it to a vote and see what everyone thinks. You'll go along with the majority opinion.

(C) Sure it's a good plan and you know damn well it's going to work. Why not get the credit? It's a chance worth taking. You speak up for the plan very strongly and swing the rest over to your viewpoint.

The Lovers

You've been going together for three months and you're both ready to take the next step. "We'll move in together and try it out," you decide. If we can live together—well, who knows? Marriage may still be a viable situation in these days. The only problem is, your place or mine? Where do we live? Your would-be roommate says, "My place is best. Location-wise, rent-wise, size-wise. Let's be wise and live there."

(A) Considering all the angles, your roommate-to-be may be right. You decide to give it a try and move all your stuff over.

(B) Let's not rush into things. Maybe the roommate-to-be's place is better, but there are other factors to consider. You've been in your apartment a long time and your roots are there. Let's make a list of pros and cons before you toss a coin to decide.

(C) What do you mean, your place is best? I've been living here longer than you lived there, and there's a lot to be said for this place. It has some comforts that yours hasn't, and it's location is better for me. If any sacrifices are to be made, let's both make them. Rent and size are not all important. Now this is a better neighborhood . . .

Who Dominates Whom?

Again, the scoring is similar to that in the interior-exterior test. The person who tends to follow the (A) mode of behavior is the least dominant, the one most likely to be persuaded by someone else, the person most uncomfortable with power. The (C) type is the most dominant, the person most apt to be on top of any situation and, of course, the person who will go after power whenever possible. The great majority of people still fall into the (B) or middle category. They will accept power, but will not go after it. They resist dominance by others, but rarely try to be dominant themselves.

Aggression or Assertiveness

We have covered two elements of the typical strong power profile: an exterior personality and the ability and desire to dominate a situation. The true power-seeker must also have a good amount of aggression—or assertiveness, whichever word pleases you. Basically, they are the same personality trait. How we view that trait determines our label for it, assertiveness or aggression. The label becomes a subtle form of editorializing, but whatever we choose to call it, the person who is comfortable with power must have it. Again a series of questions should help you to be objective about your own degree of aggression or assertiveness.

The Movie Line

It's a great flick, and you've been waiting for weeks for it to come to town. Now it's here and you go down to the box office and get your ticket then join the line and what a line it is! Right around the block. It must be a sensational film! Then, while you turn to ask the person behind you what he's heard about it, some joker cuts into line ahead of you.

(A) You're really ticked off, but what the hell. You're close enough to the front of the line to be sure of a seat and why make a fuss? It'll just create an uncomfortable situation. Better to forget it.

(B) Sure, there are plenty of seats, and it probably doesn't make any difference, but why should a guy like that get away with it. You don't say anything to him directly, but in a carrying voice you tell the person behind you that bucking the line is a pretty cheap trick, and you thought most people wouldn't do it.

(C) "That's a hell of a note," you think, and you tap him on the shoulder and say, "Look. I was here first. If you want to buck the line, get in behind me, if they'll let you, but no way are you cutting me out."

The Waiter with the Water

You're in a restaurant with a friend and after the waiter takes your order, you ask him for a glass of water. He starts serving the meal without getting you the water, and again you ask him for it. Again he forgets and by now it becomes obvious that his attitude is very unpleasant. Finally, and gracelessly, he brings the water when you've quite lost your appetite for it.

(A) You're really burned up by all this, but who wants to make a scene in a restaurant. When you're finished, to show how you feel, you leave a very small tip.

(B) You don't wait for the meal to be served.

Once you understand that this waiter is unpleasant and giving you minimal service, you get up and walk out of the restaurant.

(C) You tell the waiter off in no uncertain terms and demand to see the manager. When he comes you explain the situation and ask for an apology and another waiter.

The New Neighbors

The empty house next door has finally been sold and the new family have moved in and seems fairly settled. They appear to be about your age and your kind of people.

(A) You wait for some natural situation to occur, a situation that will allow you to meet them casually.

(B) You set up a small neighborhood party and some close friends, perhaps a weekend cocktail party, and you invite the new people with the other neighbors. Afterwards you can all compare notes and see if they're your kind of people.

(C) Once the van has gone and the curtains are up, you walk over with a bottle of wine and introduce yourself and then welcome them to the neighborhood.

The Bus Ride

You get on a city bus and not only are all the seats taken, but the aisles are filled with standees. By stretching your neck, however, you can see that the back of the bus is almost empty.

(A) You realize that pushing to the back is going to be just as uncomfortable as standing in the front, so rather than upset everyone including yourself, you hang on with the crowd in front. You haven't all that far to ride, and with so many people pressing against you, at least you can't fall over!

(B) People are getting off at the middle of the bus and you realize that with a bit of squirming you can, with each stop, get a bit closer to the rear and those empty seats.

(C) You grit your teeth and push through the crowded front of the bus, either ignoring the hostile looks and remarks or answering in kind. "Why not be sensible and move to the rear?" At the back, you relax and enjoy the elbow room you've won.

The Roadhog

You're driving along the new superhighway when some clown in a souped-up sports car whips past and cuts right in front of you, forcing you to jam on your brakes and be thankful you're wearing your seatbelt.

(A) You figure he must have had you in his blind spot, and you slow down, wishing to hell the road had six lanes so you could stay to the far right and avoid any incidents like this.

(B) You curse him out roundly as you let up on the accelerator and let him get far ahead. Who wants anything to do with a driver as stupid as that?

(C) Five minutes later, when you have a clear

64

lane available, you step on the gas and challenge him by slipping past and cutting back in front of him.

Scoring Your Aggression

A tendency to pick the last response, (C) is a sign of a high degree of aggression. If you feel most comfortable with the (A) solutions, then you can be reasonably sure that power is not something you'll be happy with. Again, the great mass of people will fit into the middle category (B). They have some degree of aggression, but it does not dominate their lives. They can handle power, but they don't need it or go after it.

Wearing the Leadership Mantle

The fourth and final trait necessary for the man who lives comfortably with a strong power profile is the quality of leadership. Traditionally, people with a drive towards power are happiest leading the flock. This doesn't mean that an interior person who wants no power is content to be led. He may be unhappy with his boss or his political leader and fight him without wanting to take over the job himself. A personal distaste for power doesn't always mean a knuckling under to power.

The important thing to remember about all these little tests and categories is that mankind does not come in standard black and white models. We are available in all shades of grey. We can have a little drive towards power or a moderate drive, no drive at all or an overwhelming drive. And to add to the classification difficulty, we are all prone to change. The man who has always been able to do without power may get a taste of real power and abuse it or the man who has thrived on power may suddenly see it all as an illusion without any inner rewards and turn away from it.

Our tests are not definitive, but they will help you towards some self-understanding. Let's look at the final one, trying on the leadership mantle.

The Boss

You work for a moderately large corporation in an executive position, and you have just come from a meeting with the boss. He's outlined the goals of the company for the coming year, and as you listen to him you realize the terrific strain he's under to achieve those goals. Alone in your office, you begin to recap the meeting.

(A) That man has a bitch of a job, you decide, and he's welcome to it. Who needs that kind of pressure? You're happy working at your own level.

(B) There is no doubt that the boss works too hard, and is it all that good for the company? He should relax and let some of the other staff take on some of the pressure.

(C) That is one tough worker and I feel for him. Someday, when I get to his position, I'll probably have to go through the same routine. There must be some techniques I could learn now that would make things easier for me then.

The Method

Someone in your department who works under you has come up with a promising but untried method for doing one of the important jobs. He sends you a memo about it.

(A) You don't really know whether or not the method will work, so you just thank him for the idea and ignore it.

(B) The method is interesting, but why take a chance with something new when what you're doing works. Still, if it's promising, others should examine it. You pass it on to the higher-ups.

(C) The method, you realize, may help your department and also help you. You decide to look into it yourself and perhaps implement it.

The Order

You are working in a local organization in a responsible position and someone above you gives an order you're in doubt about. How do you react?

(A) The very fact that they are above you indicates that the order is correct and you carry it out.

(B) Talk over the order with your superior, discuss the pros and cons, and finally agree to carry it out.

(C) You're not at all sure that this is the best way to handle the sitution, and you tell him so. Now this is the way you should like it done . . .

The Risk

The company you work for has just taken a risky step by buying a small outfit with poor sales but a big potential. You are asked by one of your co-workers what you think of the move. How do you answer him?

(A) It may work out if we're lucky, but it's a big gamble.

(B) Even if we fall on our butts, if should be a valuable experience.

(C) It's an absolutely correct step. To succeed in the business world today, you have to be prepared to take risks.

A Job Well Done

You're doing volunteer work for a political leader and one of the people under you has just done a great job on a pamphlet. What do you say to her?

(A) You tell her how good it was, but you also point out how much better it could have been if she had done thus and so.

(B) You take her aside and tell her it was a great job and it probably helped the campaign more than any other piece of literature produced.

(C) You praise her for the work she'd done, and then you go on to tell her just why you thought it was so good.

Your Score

Like the other tests, the (C) reaction is the one that indicates that you have the highest power potential.

It suggests that you have good leadership qualities, you are willing to take chances and you know how to handle people and how to react when you are in charge.

Prescott's Problem

You have taken the four tests and you have discovered, to your pleasure or dismay, depending on your attitude, that you are filled to the brim with the power motive. You are a born leader, but you are not leading. What has gone wrong?

You may have the same problem as my friend, Prescott. He's 46, good at his job and making a decent salary. He lives comfortably with his wife and two children in a house in the suburbs, yet he has an uneasy feeling of dissatisfaction.

"I think you could say I'm unfulfilled," he told me recently. "Or it may be that I'm displaced in time. I should have been a medieval despot or a revolutionary hero."

"But aren't they on opposite sides of the fence?"

He shrugged. "It's not important to me who I side with. I could be a despotic revolutionary leader or a benevolent despot—the important thing is that I wish I were a leader of men. You know, I didn't even qualify for the army. I was too young for Korea and too old for Vietnam. A shame, because I always fancied myself a war hero."

Intrigued by Prescott's fantasies, I let him take the set of power tests, and I was not too surprised to discover that he had an extremely high power motive.

"A lot of good it does me," he said, staring at

the test results. "So I'm a straight (C) on your scale, a man who should have power. Where do I get it in my situation? My job? It's a family-owned outfit. All the power is locked into the brothers who own it—and a few cousins. My home? Who wants to be petty tyrant in his own house? I've missed the army and I never had the opportunity to go into politics. You know, I think my life's a waste of good talent."

In a way, Prescott was right. His talent was power, but a situation in which he might make use of power had never arisen for him. His dilemma started me thinking. Is power situational? Or is it the property of an individual? Are there some people who will rise above their situation and become powerful, or will they, like Prescott, be crippled if the proper situation never arises?

In an overall view of society, do the circumstances make the leader? But even if this is so, only certain people must be capable of taking advantage of those circumstances. If the right circumstances ever presented themselves to Prescott, he could become a leader. True, but failing this, was he doomed to be relegated to the powerless role he now played?

A possible answer to Prescott's problem has been suggested by the work of Dr. G. A. Talland reported in the *Journal of Abnormal Social Psychology* back in 1954. He studied men and women who exerted power in psychotherapeutic groups and eventually became leaders. Granted that they had the ability to handle power—how did they get it? Was it by sensing the opinion of the group and going along with that opinion, or was it that their ideas happened to be close to the ideas of the group?

Neither of these two factors were at work, according to Dr. Talland. Careful observations of group dynamics convinced him that the successful leaders were able to gradually change the group's ideas to fit their own. It was less a case of taking advantage of a situation to become a leader than of changing the situation to fit their leadership. They were strongly motivated in terms of power, and although the groups they moved into had established leaders, they were still able to take power away from the others and become the new leaders.

When you consider what these men did, Prescott's excuse of living in the wrong time doesn't hold up. For some reason, in spite of his high power potential, he didn't try hard enough to become a leader. Another man would have changed jobs, or found some area where his strength could be used. Another man would somehow have changed the situation to suit his needs. A difficult job? Well, consider little Tommy's takeover.

Tommy's Takeover

The ability to use power is something that we are either born with or we learn very early in life. Take Tommy, a four-year-old who was entered in a play group by his working mother. Tommy very quickly became a leader of the group, but then his family moved and a year later, at five, Tommy was put into another play group in mid-session.

For a while Tommy was displaced, low man on the new group's totem pole. But instead of accepting his lack of status, Tommy studied the situation carefully. Playing with the other children, he learned the schedule of activities, then he very gradually began to give orders, to tell the other children what to do—and they always obeyed him.

A born leader? A powerful personality? Perhaps. But what Tommy actually did was to order the other children to do *what they were already doing* or *what they were going to do next anyway*. The chances of their disobeying his orders were slim.

Once he established his right to give these orders and be obeyed, he began to make slight changes in the accepted routine, to insist that everyone should use red crayons to color a lady's dress, and blue crayons for a man's suit, or he would hurry things up. "We have to finish all our clay work by two o'clock!" The changes were always simple, things no one cared much about, and gradually Tommy's way was adopted.

Once he had come this far, Tommy took a final step. He announced that he owned certain important things in the play group, all the crayon sets, the scissors, the paste pots. But he never monopolized his ownership. He graciously gave each object back to the boy or girl who had it before Tommy announced his possession. He never took physical possession of any of these things, and everyone who used them continued to use them, but very subtly the right to use them came to be Tommy's disposition.

By the end of the term Tommy was the undisputed leader of the group. He had managed successfully to take power into his own hands. He made the decisions for the group and gave the orders, real orders now, not simple confirmations of what everyone was doing. Tommy had risen above the situation, or he had created his own situation to take over power.

The way adults assume and keep power is often similar to the technique Tommy used. Within an organization, adults with the equivalent of Tommy's power drive, manipulated their own position and the position and opinions of others to get control.

If people are subtle and clever in their manipulations and we like them, we think of them as charismatic, especially when they operate in politics. If we don't like them, and their methods are blatant, we usually call them unscrupulous or cunning. But when the charisma or dressing is stripped away, both methods seem to be the same. These are people who need power, who thrive on it, go after it and manipulate others to get it. Their power profile is high, but so is their power motive.

3

THE SOURCES OF POWER

Verbal Games

In the last chapter we met Tommy and saw his surprising ability to cope with displacement and take over leadership. Tommy was only five-years-old, yet he already had the ability to wield power, and he knew how to go about getting it. Where does such talent come from? Was Tommy born with it, or did he learn it?

Let's consider Tommy before the age of four, and let's also consider Mark, one of the other children in Tommy's play group. Mark looks a lot like Tommy—a tow-headed little boy, stocky, with a round face and an alert air. But their personalities are very different. Tommy is a leader. Mark is a follower. Tommy can take rejection, but seldom gets it because he assumes he'll be accepted. Mark takes for granted that he'll be rejected. Mark cries readily, rarely asks for things and never demands them. Already, he is somewhat of a loser in the game of life. Tommy, on the other hand, uses great assurance to demand and get what he assumes is his right.

Tommy grew up in a middle-class family with parents who were well educated, who were delighted to have a baby boy and seemed never to tire of playing with their child. "He's really remarkable," Tommy's father used to say proudly, holding Tommy on his lap. "Look at the way he follows my hand, and at four weeks! How about that?" He would lean forward and say, "Goo, goo, goo!" and Tommy would gurgle happily.

It was their favorite game, and it persisted all through the baby's infancy. Tommy's father would pick him up as soon as he got home from work, set him in his lap and begin playing with him. He'd make funny sounds, and Tommy would imitate them. Then he would imitate Tommy's sounds.

"He really enjoys him," Tommy's mother would say as she watched her husband. "Look at the two of them, a grown man and a baby gurgling back and forth." She didn't like to admit that she played the same games when she was alone with the baby. After all, he was a delight and certainly something special.

"Did you ever see a kid as responsive as Tommy?" his father would ask proudly. "Listen to him. Not even a year old and he's already saying words—listen!"

By two, Tommy was so alert, so responsive, that even objective outsiders had to agree with his adoring father. He was a very special child.

Mark, the "loser," grew up not far from Tommy, but in not as nice a neighborhood. His parents too were different. Although they were able to send him to the same play group, they were far from middle-class. Mark's father worked for a building contractor and his mother clerked in the local supermarket. They both had to work hard in order to keep their heads above the economic waters, and although Mark's father loved him every bit as much as Tommy's father loved him, there was no playing around in the evenings.

For one thing, Mark's father came home exhausted after work. He had all he could do to read the evening papers without dozing off, and after supper he spent a few mesmerized hours before bed watching TV. Mark's mother raced home from her job at the supermarket to relieve the babysitter and prepare supper for her husband. Mark was loved, but there was little time for his parents to show any of that love. During his early months he received attention only when he needed it. He was well-fed, his diapers were changed, and that was about it.

Aside from his physical exhaustion at the end of the day, Mark's father could never have played those "silly" verbal games with a baby. "A grown man making goo-goo noises? It's sickening," he said when he saw one of his friends doing it. "A kid has to learn to stand on his own feet and become a man. How can you expect him to grow up straight if you play those stupid baby games? You leave a kid alone, and he'll develop self-reliance."

Mark's mother had no time to indulge her baby. The first time he wandered off she was furious with him and gave him a good hiding. His father agreed. "You've got to break a kid's will. He has to obey for his own good. Hell, we can't take the chance of his getting into trouble when we're not home."

Mark responded to punishment with obedience. When his first few attempts at independence were put down, he seemed content to play by himself for long periods of time.

When Tommy was the same age he was an alert, outgoing youngster, ready to get into any trouble that presented itself. "The boy's a born snoop," his mother laughed. "He pokes into everything and he's always exploring. I can't begin to keep him in the back yard."

Dr. Hunt's Experiments

On the surface, Tommy and Mark had been through similar childhoods. Both had been well taken care of, well-fed, well-housed, well-clothed and, best of all, well-loved. Both were wanted by their parents, and it seemed that the only obvious difference was that Tommy came from middle-class parents and Mark from working-class parents. Yet Mark's parents never stinted in the things they gave him. He had as many toys as Tommy, ate as well and eventually attended the same play group.

The difference, the very obvious difference, was in the amount of attention paid to the two children. While still a baby, Mark was treated in a very traditional manner. He wasn't played with nor was he encouraged to explore his world. Tommy, however, was played with constantly, using all sorts of ridiculous baby games, and he was rarely punished for his attempts at independence.

In many ways Tommy developed faster than Mark. He became secure, more sure of his friends and himself, more alert and more reactive. He learned how to use power and how to get ahead.

It could be argued that there must have been a basic difference between the two, a genetic difference. It's possible that Mark was born with an insecure personality, and all the verbal games in the world wouldn't have made him into a Tommy. No doubt there were genetic differences between the two, but even considering these, a great part of Tommy's confidence and assurance came from his parental treatment, just as much of Mark's insecurity came from his.

Dr. J. McVicker Hunt, professor emeritus of psychology at the University of Illinois, firmly believes that you can raise the levels of intellectual capacity in most children. To prove this, he started a study at an orphanage in Iran before the recent revolution. The children there seemed so retarded that the two-year-olds could not sit up, and most of the four-year-olds could not walk. The standard orphanage treatment of these children was to feed them and clothe them, but to leave them alone. There was no playing, no talking, no cuddling, no show of affection. The understaffed orphanage had no time for any of that.

Dr. Hunt did many experiments with these orphans, but his most rewarding results came when he started playing verbal games with a group of infants, imitating their gurgles and coos, shifting from one sound to another, then naming parts of their bodies as he touched them. These children, he reported, became so alert, so responsive, so attractive in fact, that the adoption rate (in a Moslem country adoption is rare) rose from less than four percent to over sixty percent.

A Cleveland psychiatrist, who introduced me to Dr. Hunt's work, explained that in these children there was not only a rise in alertness and responsiveness, but also a rise in leadership and assertiveness. "And you can readily link both of those—leadership and assertiveness—to power," he said. "Children who are talked to, played with and taught to respond to simple verbal games in infancy, also seem to become more intelligent."

I questioned that, but he was very firm. "They can be raised over thirty points on a standard intelligence scale," he insisted. "We know that most children reared in orphanages, like those Hunt studied in Iran, have a fifty-point drop in intelligence. Is it surprising that by challenging these babies and children with games and play we can raise them thirty points? If we were to start them off in one of the best educational day care centers a few months after birth, we'd get damned close to a one hundred-point rise—and then where's the genetic difference?"

He considered that for a moment, then added thoughtfully, "There is certainly some genetic differences among children. Some are born smarter or more outgoing than others, but I believe you can do wonders within the limits of these differences. By enriching a child's early life with games and play, you can increase that child's chances of becoming bright, powerful, and a leader not only during childhood, but also when he becomes an adult."

Tommy was an enriched child. Mark was quite the opposite, a deprived child, deprived of any exciting early stimuli. But in the same play group where Tommy led and Mark lagged, there were all kinds of children. There were a few who constantly challenged Tommy for leadership, and a few who, like Mark, did as they were told and faded imperceptibly into the background.

The greater number of children in the group

were boys and girls who, while they had no great desire to lead, still were not content to follow blindly. They took Tommy's measure constantly, and allowed him to lead as long as he demonstrated his leadership. They went along with the rest of the group, but had the potential for independence.

Most of us in adult life are like that. We follow our leaders as long as they demonstrate leadership and we continue to believe in them. When belief falters, we follow grudgingly if we must, or, if we can, we try to change our leadership.

We have seen that the early stimulation of a child helps to make a leader, but this is only one element in leadership. The parent's relationship to the child as well as the child's relationship to the parents, to any brothers or sisters and to the outside world are some of the many other elements that shape personality and affect first the child's and then the adult's struggle for power.

One important factor in the development of the child is the distribution of power within the family. Who rules the roost, and who becomes the role model for the child? Whom can the child look up to and follow? Since each of us is different, each will react in a slightly different way to the same situation. The autocratic, domineering father may make a rebellious, power-hungry adult out of one child, and a compliant, passive adult out of another. We are all born with different strengths and weaknesses over and beyond those imposed on us by the environment. Another child, exposed to the same verbal play that influenced Tommy, might not have grown up to become a leader, though he would certainly have become a brighter, more outgoing and alert person than he would have been without the verbal play.

Table Politics

In any family there is usually one person who holds the reins of power. It can be a domineering mother or a manipulative father. Spend a day observing the family, and you can usually tell who the leader is. But there are quicker ways. A glance at how the family seats itself at the dinner table may give a clue.

A rectangular table has an interchangeable head and foot. The more domineering parent will usually sit at the head of the table. Let's assume that it's the father. Then where does mother sit? If she accepts her husband's power and if the relationship between them is good, she will usually sit catercorner to his right or left. If there is one child, he or she will sit across from the mother. This usually spells a harmonious family.

If there is some tension between the husband and wife, a struggle for power within the family, the same rectangular table can become a small battlefield. The wife, whose husband has assumed the dominant seat at the head of the table, may challenge his authority by deciding to sit at the other end. Since head and foot, applied to the table, are relative terms, the foot may become the head, the power spot, depending on the strength of either contestant.

What is unusual about these power struggles is the fact that they are completely unconscious. The wife does not take a seat at the foot of the table in a deliberate effort to challenge her husband. It is just that her choosing to sit there becomes the spatial expression of a power struggle within the family.

As far as children go, if there are two or three, their arrangement around the table often conforms to unwritten laws. As a rule, the oldest boy will sit at his mother's side, staking a claim on her in a Freudian challenge to his father. The oldest girl will take a position to her father's left or right. The other children must scramble for places depending on the interfamily pecking order. Again, all of this is done unconsciously, and there are always exceptions. One classic problem that can make all of these struggles invalid is the location of the door to the kitchen. This must be convenient for the wife (assuming she does the cooking), and it can play hell with any power struggle.

Another potential power block is the shape of the table. A round table makes a struggle for power difficult, as King Arthur recognized when he let Merlin tout him into using one. But even with a round table, things quickly fall into place. Wherever Arthur sat became the head of the table, and in power-oriented families, wherever the most powerful member sits turns into the head of the table.

An interesting sidelight on table politics comes from the jury room. Social scientists used to wonder how juries selected their foreman. They did some experimenting and discovered that when the jury filed in and sat down to choose their foreman, whoever was at the "head" of the table was usually selected.

This finding was intriguing enough to make them wonder who took this position of power, since jury members were not assigned definite seats. They found that it boiled down to a question of power. The most powerful people on the jury, powerful in terms of money and position, automatically sat at the head of the table. They were doctors, bankers, industrialists, politicians, businessmen. They understood that their position gave them the right to the seat of power, and in turn the other members of the jury understood that whoever sat in those seats had power. Again, it was something unconscious, done without the kind of planning that says, "I am important, so I'll sit in an important and powerful spot."

Sometimes it is fun to play the power game in any "long table" situation. I have been invited to meetings in conference rooms with long tables, and I have found that getting to that power seat before the real leader does can throw the meeting into some confusion, especially when only a few people are gathered at one end of the table. The real leader, knowing where he should sit, is usually too polite to ask you to change, and yet too uncomfortable in a subordinate position to conduct a proper meeting. The kind thing to do, once you have had your fun, is to suggest that you'd be more comfortable if you changed places.

The Wonder Child

In any family we have assumed that age goes along with power, and that the most powerful person, the real leader, is the mother or father. But the truth is, age doesn't always give power. Grandparents, sharing a household, are often stripped of their power they once had as family heads. If they are given the head or foot of the table, it's more as a courtesy, a gesture of grace, rather than an admission of real power, and it's usually only done when they come to visit. If they "live in" they must enter the same power struggle as the rest of the family. Sometimes a crusty old grandparent will win the power position, especially if there is enough money behind him.

A surprising power focus in many families is not in either parent or grandparent, but in one of the children. In the Hamilton family, it was John, the oldest boy. There were four Hamilton children, John Jr. was fifteen, Laura, eleven, Peter eight and Michael six. John Sr., the father, was a hard-working man, a meat packer. His wife, Carol, had gone back to work temporarily as a secretary during some hard economic times. The "temporarily," however, stretched out, and in effect the children were without both parents for most of the day.

It was during this period that John Jr. took over the reins of power. It began with little things, preparing his sister's and brother's lunches, checking out their clothes, and making sure that they did their homework. Then it went on to bigger things, to having dinner ready when his parents came home, to assigning chores to the younger children, to making sure that they obeyed the house rules and kept their rooms clean, their clothes in order, and finally to supervising the shopping and doling out allowances.

"I don't know what I'd do without Junior," his mother told all her friends. "He's responsible for the whole house running smoothly, and with all that he's at the top of his class in school."

There was nothing of the martyr about John Jr., nor was there anything of the tyrant. He ran a tight ship, but a fair one. He wouldn't let Laura or Peter bully little Michael, but he also insisted that Michael toe the line. He had the power in the family, but he handled it gracefully.

Gradually, over the years, John Jr.'s role as head of the family became entrenched. He went through college on a scholarship and was accepted, again on scholarship, at a prestigous law school. During all those years he arbitrated disputes in the family, advised and helped his brothers, supported his sister through an unhappy love affair and saw her safely married. He refused to let his parents speculate on a chancy stock deal, and he convinced them that they should invest in some very profitable real estate.

Even after John Jr. married, he remained the family head. No decisive family move was made without his advice and yet, in spite of his power, he was never resented by the others. "I don't have to ask John before I do something," his brother Michael explained to his girlfriend when he first brought her to a family dinner. "But it's just—well, I know his advice is good and I wouldn't want to do anything he was against."

I spoke to Dr. Avodah Offit, a New York City psychiatrist, about people like John Jr. "Is it an unusual phenomenon for someone like John to become the most powerful member of a family, the one the entire family leans on and, in a sense, exploits?"

"It's wrong to think of it as exploitation," she said, "or of anybody being used. John is in a position of power because he wants to be there. He has the peculiar type of makeup that is most comfortable handling power and using it wisely. He helps the family survive, and they in turn help him.''

"If he does everything for them, how do they help him?''

"By bolstering his ego. By giving him love, affection, respect. By adding an extra dimension of meaning to his life. Your John is what, in the literature, is called the *wunderkind,* the wonderchild, the gifted, beloved one on whom all responsibility falls. It's not uncommon. Many families have a child like that, someone who, for one reason or another, takes over from his parents. It may be that the parents haven't the strength necessary to run a family, or perhaps it's a matter of time, as it was with John Jr.'s family. Circumstances prevented them from being full-time parents. They were both working parents. There was a void, and John stepped in.''

I nodded thoughtfully. "In my own family, the wonderchild was my oldest brother. He wasn't quite as dedicated as John, but my mother died when we were very young and Jerry took over. He advised us, disciplined us and even took some of my father's financial troubles on his own shoulders, and he was comfortable with all that power. He neither resented it nor misused it.''

Dr. Offit nodded. "Usually the one who becomes the wonderchild manages the role adroitly. It's interesting that usually, but not always, the oldest child steps into the role. In many cases, the mantle of power is passed on from the oldest to the younger child.

"Is there a struggle to get the role, a power struggle?''

"Very rarely. But that may be because the wonderchild handles the power so well. He—or she—works for the benefit of the family, not for his own benefit, and this becomes obvious to the other family members."

The Baby Tug-of-War

It struck me that this was one of the very few cases, in or out of the family, where power was acquired and held without a struggle. Because of this there is no need for the wonderchild to resort to any obnoxious power games, to become a bully or a martyr or to arouse guilt in the other family members.

"I'm very aware of the kind of struggle for power that can go on in a typical family," Dr. Offit told me. "I remember a part of it from my own early days as a mother.

"When my first child was born, my husband and I were as thrilled as any young parents, and we decided that the one thing we would never do was get involved in any of the power games we knew about. Common sense and what was best for the baby would rule our lives.

"Then my husband's mother came to visit and looked at my sleeping child in dismay. 'He's on his stomach!'

"'That's the way he likes to sleep,' I explained.

"'But you mustn't allow it,' she said firmly and, reaching down, turned the baby onto his back. 'On his stomach, his nose will get all scrunched up. It could affect his breathing.' She straightened his sleeves and smiled with pleasure. 'There, the little darling!'

"And that afternoon my mother came to visit her new grandson. She clucked appreciatively until I put him down for his nap in the position my mother-in-law had advised. 'Not on his back!' my mother cried out.

" 'Why not?'

" 'Are you mad? No baby should sleep on his back. It can cause all sorts of deformities. Listen to that breathing! Here, let me turn him. The little angel!'

"She turned him around firmly and he lay like that till my mother-in-law came and, just as firmly, turned him on his back. That went on for over a week, and I grew haggard with anxiety, turning the baby from one position to another as soon as each visit ended. I was caught in the middle of a classic power game.

"What was going on," Dr. Offit smiled, "Was a perfect example of a power struggle, but it wasn't the kind of power your wonderchild exerts. Each grandmother wanted to dominate the situation, to dictate what was correct—but not necessarily for the baby's good."

"That kind of power," I said, "is what the dictionary defines as swaying power, the power to influence someone, to get your own way."

"I would call it identification power," Dr. Offit said. "You have the power if you can get someone to identify with you. It's the power we see in charismatic individuals who can sway audiences. Many preachers and politicians seem to have it. There is almost a mystical quality to it. Reverend Jim Jones, who commanded all those people to commit suicide, had that sort of power."

Later, thinking over the difference between the

power of the typical wonderchild and the charismatic power Dr. Offit talked of, I could see how each followed one of the dictionary's two definitions. The power to do things, the power of ability, is what the wonderchild has. I choose to call it creative power. It is a postive source of power, and we all have some amount of it, or can have some if we try. It's the power of talent, the power an artist or a fine craftsman has, the power of a good worker, a competent teacher, a caring parent or a loving child. It is the power that comes from ability, from a job well done, from the willingness to do something, whether that something is as far out as crossing the Atlantic in a balloon or as ordinary as cooking a meal. They are both creative acts in the sense that they use a talent, an ability within us.

This is positive power, and it is always good, always constructive.

Opposed to it is manipulative power, the power that Dr. Offit called identification power. This is the power to sway another person, to bend him to your will, to convince him to do your bidding. It can be achieved with charisma, but it can also be achieved by emotional manipulation. In a family a parent becomes manipulative by using guilt to sway a child, a wife by using martyrdom to sway a husband, a lover by withholding approval. Very often the weakest member of a family will resort to manipulative power by using his very helplessness.

A combination of arousing guilt and self-martyrdom is essential for this kind of manipulation. The manipulator says, "I am small and helpless while you are strong and powerful. The imbalance is due to some fault of yours, and there is a debt you owe me because of it."

The proper response is, "I did not cause your helplessness, so no debt exists." But very few of us can take that position, or if we do we are still subject to a nagging guilt because of our own strength and our innate sense of fairness.

Legitimate and Coercive Power

In addition to the two opposite sources of social power, creative and manipulative, there are four other power sources in our society. One is *legitimate power*, the power of the law, the power that must be obeyed if we are to live together in a civilized community. The most obvious source of this power is the police. On an international scale, it is the state and the military.

Legitimate power is legal power, and if we are proper, dues-paying citizens it protects us. If we are out to harm the community it persecutes us. In a very real sense legitimate power is absolute. "You can't fight City Hall," is an accurate expression of its strength. The government is a part of legitimate power, but in its eddies and backwaters it gives rise to the swamp of bureaucracy. Legitimate power becomes perverted in these swamps, and instead of protecting the interests of the citizens, it protects the interests of the bureaucracy itself. The citizen comes to be a thorn in the bureaucracy's side, and he finds himself caught in an irresistible quicksand of red tape. The very power that was set up to help him defeats him and sucks him under.

Bureaucracy comes into being when the people who wield legitimate power begin to change from the creative aspects of such power to the manipulative aspects. The power becomes a self-perpetuating attempt to keep the bureaucracy in power, and only incidentally to serve citizens. Anyone who has ever attempted to collect unemployment insurance, receive Medicaid benefits or even argue with the Internal Revenue Service knows the power of such a bureaucracy.

A fourth type of power that often rises in response to legitimate power is *coercive power*. The person who places himself outside the law must resort to coercive power as a means of fighting legitimate power. It is the power of the weapon, whether the weapon be a knife, a gun or superior strength. Coercive power probably started back in the stone age when a caveman used a handy rock to bash in the skull of a neighbor and take away his wife and possessions.

No society could tolerate this kind of behavior and continue to survive, so legitimate power was set up to oppose it. But in all the years since, coercive power has never been overcome to any appreciable degree. Indeed, as civilization increased in complexity, so coercive power became better organized and more powerful. In the old days, the man who initiated coercive power, who first smashed in his neighbor's skull, usually ended up as leader of the tribe. His coercive power was legitimized.

Later, in historical times, it was a common occurrence for the strongest robber baron to end up as a rightful ruler, and even today we find that the Mafia, an extremely organized group using coercive power, is working its way into the legitimate institutions of our society. Once coercive power becomes strong enough, it sets out to become legitimate.

Coercive power can also exist within the family. It's not uncommon for one child to set himself up as the family bully and, with the weapon of superior strength, force his brothers and sisters to do as he wants. Parents too can, and do, use coercive power on their children with spankings and beatings, or on each other. The battered wife is as familiar as the battered child, and there have been reports of battered husbands and battered parents as well.

Reward Power and Group Power

The fifth type of power is *reward power*. This is the power you possess when you are in a position to reward someone with money or favors, but it is usually a two-way street. The worker rewards the boss with a job well done, while the boss, in turn, rewards the worker with a salary. The power, however, is weighted on the side of the boss. He is usually able to dictate terms of employment and salary, especially when there is a large, available labor force.

Reward power exists on every level. The man who rewards his mistress with an expensive gift is using the power to get his own way, just as the parent who rewards her child with a kiss is using reward power to get what she wants.

For reward power to work properly, the reward must be something desired or needed by the other party, desired so much he will agree to the power demands in order to get it. In prehistoric times the tribe with the most power was the one that owned the most desired commodities, whether it was meat, fish, salt, ceramics or iron.

In modern times we have developed a monetary system so that the reward can be uniform—money. The more money you have, the more potential power you possess, for money can be used as a reward on any level.

When the reward becomes more elusive, when it is affection, praise, a favor—the power too becomes elusive. You are only as powerful as the need for your qualities. There is power in the ability to love, to praise or to help someone. If no one wants your love or praise, the real power you possess shrinks. But someone always wants money, and the power that resides in money is universal and constant.

A sixth power, *group power*, has come about as an answer to reward power. It is the power of union, the power that comes when a lot of people with the same needs and desires get together to help each other. In a work situation, the boss may offer the reward of a salary, but if there are more workers than he needs, he can set that salary at a subsistence level, and it will still be reward enough for him to wield power.

But with group power, the workers can form a union to get enough power to reach their goal, whether it's a higher-than-subsistence wage or shortened hours or better working conditions. With group power, consumers can find the strength to demand that the rewards for their money, the commodities they buy, be worth the price they pay. The commodities, whether they be a home, a car or a suit of clothes, are rewards, and whoever produces them has the power to demand money for them. Group power gives the buyer the right to demand a satisfactory product. We label it *consumer power*, just as we label the ability to fight legitimate power *voter power*. Both are examples of group power.

The Power of Responsibility

There are perversions possible with all kinds of power; by its very nature power is prone to corruption. Even creative power can be subverted. The teacher who uses her knowledge creatively to teach can also use that knowledge to humiliate or shame her students. The artist can use his knowledge as propaganda to persuade people, and the scientist can use his abilities to create deadly weapons. Legitimate power can be misused not only when it turns into bureaucracy, but also to grant special favors—to become, in fact, reward power within the legitimate framework. Reward power is often misused, and even group power can be misused by one group to get an unfair advantage over another or to exclude undesirables outside the group. Group pressure among children, peer pressure, is often used against each other, forcing them into group behavior, and sometimes it is used against the parents. Everyone else is doing it. Can't I?

Understanding the different varieties of power allows you to understand your own need for power. Some have an insatiable appetite for it, while others are content with just enough to make life comfortable. Some of us crave the charismatic type of power, the ability to sway and influence others, while still others yearn for creative power. Some people are happiest with legitimate power, while others find that life under legitimate power is unbearable, for them, coercive power, crime, is the only answer. Some want money for the reward power it can bring, and others find their satisfaction in group power, in joining others to control the power leveled against them.

I know two men who are writers, both with a touch of creative genius. One has devoted himself to what he calls "good writing"—short stories and novels, none of them popular, none of them best-sellers. He publishes his short stories in small magazines with a lot of prestige and small budgets, and his novels are usually put out by offbeat publishers in small editions. He struggles along financially and supports himself by teaching at a local college.

"But I have what I want," he told me. "I walk into a gathering of writers and critics, and they all know my work. The public doesn't know much about me, but the people who count, in my opinion, respect me. They look up to me."

"But is there any power in that?" I asked.

"Power? Of course. There's the power of recognition from people I admire and who admire me. That's the power I want out of life."

The other writer I know appeals to a different audience. He too is creative, but his talent lies in a different type of writing. His books are about adventure, romance, sex. His audience is much wider. He is usually on the best-seller list, but he isn't popular with critics and other writers.

"Power?" He shrugged. "Power lies in money. I'm paid very well and I can do what I please. The freedom that money gives me, the power to go anyplace or do anything is reward enough. In all honesty, I couldn't care less what the critics say. I'm not interested in critical acclaim or the recognition of other writers. Give me a good movie sale, and I don't give a damn if the literary elite ignores me."

Both men have valid goals, and each is aware of the type of power he wants. The writer who is after literary acclaim doesn't consider that he's made a sacrifice by giving up any handsome royalties. He feels he's gaining a great deal by the recognition of his peers. Nor does the bestselling author feel he has lost out because the critics ignore him. His sales are the power he wants.

The same dichotomy of power exists between the artist who does commercial art and the one who is willing to let the profits go and concentrate on fine art alone; between the manufacturer who produces a fine product for a small clientele and the one who turns out a cheap product for the masses. This contrast exists on almost every level of creative work.

Occasionally the craftsman is discovered, the writer of "good" stories becomes a best-seller and the fine artist begins selling canvasses at exalted prices. But more often the power these people have remains the power of responsibility.

Each of them feels a responsibility to his craft, whether that craft is artistic or mundane, whether it is a special job or a routine job. Linked to all creative power is the power of responsibility, the power that comes from doing your work to the best of your ability.

When that power is combined with creative power, the need for reward power is lessened. The artist who is convinced of his own talent and who follows that talent gets reward enough in the experience of his craft.

The same gratification of responsibility exists on other levels, on levels where the creative power is not art or literature or craftmanship. Sometimes the creative power may not be in terms of the job, but in terms of a man's children and family.

Recently I spoke to a friend at the wedding of his youngest daughter. He had a modest income because in all his years of work he had never risen to the upper echelon of his company. Still, the wedding was a grand affair.

"How did you manage it?" I asked. "You must have gone for broke."

He shook his head. "*We*, how did *we* manage it. All my kids and their husbands and wives chipped in and cooked and cleaned and really made the whole affair."

"They're great kids," I said admiringly. "But then they've always been great, never in any trouble or on drugs . . . happy too. How did you do it?"

He grinned. "Hell, they were just born that way, I guess." Then he chewed his lip for a moment and in a serious voice said, "I've often thought about why the kids are so solid, and I think, oddly enough, it's because of a decision I made a long time ago. There was a point in my career when, with a little effort, a little more time, I could have gotten into management and begun the long climb up to the top. That was when my wife and I talked things over and I decided, with her behind me, that

97

I'd pass the chance by."

"Why?" I was surprised. "If it was in your own field . . ."

"Yes, I know, but if I took that one step up in the organization, my real responsibilty would be to the job. I didn't want that. I wanted my real responsibility to be my family, first and foremost. I never wanted to be in a position where they might come second."

"But it meant giving up so much."

"Only in terms of material gain. Look, I'm happy in my job. Don't get me wrong. It's just that I set limits on how much responsibility I wanted to give to my work and how much to my family. The greater amount will always go to my family, because they give me greater satisfaction." He nodded towards his two sons. "And I think it shows. They're decent kids."

He had made a choice, and from his point of view, a good one. The gratification he received from his children was as much as any creative person would get from any exertion of his talent. My friend's talent, his happiest talent, was fathering!

4

WOMAN POWER

The Shift in the Family

A recent article in *The Wall Street Journal* stressed the fact that thousands of women in the United States are taking courses and seminars that teach them how to be assertive and use power. These seminars, often very expensive, promise women that through popular theories of corporate gamesmanship and trendy motivational techniques they will learn how to get to the top of a male-dominated business world.

Women are aware of the power plays men use to get ahead in business, the article points out, and they are willing to give time and money to learn them. But it also stresses a very important fact—learning the techniques alone is not going to work. The article quotes a director of sales personnel who says that the women he sees who are graduates of these seminars "use stock phrases and ask taught, not experienced, questions."

What has happened is that women, in order to get ahead in business, are now playing the same manipulative games that men do. However, the article concludes, in spite of these seminars and training programs, the women who make it in the job market are those who concentrate on developing their skills and talents. They are the competent ones.

The woman who gets ahead in the world of business has learned the difference between manipulative and creative power, and she understands that creative power is what she will ultimately be judged by.

It is no secret that in the job world women are generally in a position of lesser power than men. This lack of business power is a reflection of the social world. While about half of all American women work in jobs outside the home, the latest available Commerce Department statistics show that only about seven percent of these women earn $15,000 or more annually. Forty percent of all men who work make salaries higher than this and hold seventy-eight percent of the managerial jobs.

Today half of all American women work. Tomorrow it may be a much greater number. Eventually there will be a shift in the relationship of power between men and women, but it will not come easy. No group in power is ever willing to give up its power.

When it does come, the shift will undoubtedly start inside the family. When a wife brings home a paycheck, she makes a declaration of her right to have a say in any family decision. If a non-working wife has such a right, it's because her husband has given it to her out of love or generosity. A working wife doesn't have to depend on male generosity. She contributes to the family fund, and her contribution entitles her to a vote on how it will be spent.

Irene and George are examples of how the balance of power can tilt once the wife begins to work. For many years, George was the moneymaker. Irene stayed home and took care of the house and kids, and they both seemed content in their roles, a very happy couple. When any decisions had to be made, where to go on vacation, what kind of car to buy—even what to have for dinner, it was always George's wishes that came first. "It just doesn't matter that much to me," Irene would say. "Besides, I'm really happiest when we're doing what you want."

When the kids started school, Irene became bored with the housewife routine. "I think I'll start doing some volunteer work with the handicapped kids at the local schools," she told George, and he thought that was a fine idea, something to keep her busy, and at least she'd be home in the early afternoon.

The volunteer work became more and more interesting, and finally Irene decided to go back to school to ger her masters degree. "I really want to work in special education," she announced, and George agreed, somewhat reluctantly. "Are you sure you can handle the house and kids?"

"A piece of cake," Irene assured him. "I've got everything down to a routine."

The routine helped and Irene made it through graduate school in record time and began to work in the local school. Everything was smooth at first, but gradually a change took place. "I guess I was the one who changed most," Irene admitted. "I wasn't quite as ready to give in to George on all the little things that 'didn't matter'—or at least they hadn't mattered while George was the breadwinner. Now I began to feel that maybe I deserved to have my way in a few things. After all, I was helping out with the money. Oh, I didn't make nearly as much as George, but still my salary let us vacation in places we couldn't afford before. Why shouldn't we go where I wanted to? And I never was happy with a manual shift in the car. Why couldn't we have an automatic now?''

It began to get out of hand, according to George. ''There was a time when Irene went out of her way to make my favorite food for dinner. Now it's only food we both like or what she has time to prepare. She can't stand math, so who has to help the kids with their homework? Me!''

''What happened,'' Irene admitted, ''is that the job changed me. You know, I did very well, and in two years I was running my department. I had to make a lot of decisions at work, important decisions, and I've learned to add up pros and cons and come up with the right answers. How could I come home and play the part of 'yes' woman? Because that's what I used to be. It was always, 'Yes, George. We'll do whatever you say.' Well, it's different now. It can't be like that anymore. Maybe I've had a taste of power, and I like it. I just think too much of myself now to go along with someone else's decisions all the time.''

George and Irene worked things out eventually, but it wasn't easy. The hardest time came when Irene was offered a job running a school for the handicapped, a very fine job with a lot of responsibility and a salary higher than George's. It also meant relocating.

''That was the toughest decision of our marriage,'' Irene told me. ''While we were trying to decide, I became unbearable to live with, hostile and withdrawn. I spent long hours at the job and neglected George and the kids, almost deliberately. I knew that the job was terrific and I wanted it more than anything else I had ever wanted. I also knew that taking it meant George had to give up his job. All I could think of was divorce. That seemed the only answer."

"What we did," George explained, "was go to a marriage counselor, a very wise lady who helped us see that this wasn't necessarily a dead end. Everything is negotiable, she assured us, as long as you love each other and trust each other.

"We both took a long, hard look at our lives and what we wanted out of them. I realized how much Irene's work had changed her, what a different person she had become—assertive, sure of herself, a very determined woman. I'm not like that. Oh, I'm not weak, but I don't go after the main chance. I began to understand that Irene's giving in to me in the early years of our marriage was a way of propping me up. A mature man shouldn't need that."

"What did you do?" I asked him.

"The sensible thing—at least I thought it was sensible and still do. I realized that Irene's job was more important than mine in every way, even the benefits were better. I took a leave of absence, got a hotel room in the town where the school that had offered her a job was located, and I went job hunting. I found something, too. Oh, not as good as my other job, but good enough. It's not an easy answer, but it's an answer we both can live with. I didn't want to lose Irene, and that was what was happening."

What was also happening was a subtle shift in family power, a shift that is going on all over the United States. In the simple husband-as-breadwinner situation, the power resides with the husband, and usually all decisions revolve around his needs, his job, his comfort and health. When the wife joins him as breadwinner, there is a shuffling of priorities. Which comes first, the family or the job? Even when both jobs are treated with equal respect, the time away from the job, the time spent at home is not. Housework, cooking, shopping, child care—all these are treated as the woman's responsibility.

Very often in such a situation the husband will make things harder by not only refusing to share the housework, but also by being overly sloppy and overly demanding. He'll complain about how his shirts are ironed, his clothes cleaned, about the meals and the childen's behavior. Such a husband is fighting a last-ditch effort to hold onto power, to make sure he still counts, is still important, still top dog—above all, still a man. He sees his wife's work as a rejection of him rather than as an aid to the family.

This type of behavior is less likely to happen if the two of them are working when they go into a marriage and keep both jobs afterward, especially if each respects the other's work.

The ultimate solution in any situation where both husband and wife work must be an equal split in power. The more equal the responsibility and decision making, the happier the marriage. The most important thing is for both partners to talk over their problems and thrash out the solutions. As George told me, "Everything is negotiable" as long as the partners love each other and care about making the marriage work.

And if, when all is said and done, the marriage

still breaks up and the answer is divorce, it is a far better situation if both partners are working. A wife without any means of support, with no financial power, is often a reason for a bad marriage.

Sarah's Scenario

Women, coming into the business world in increasing numbers, will be faced not only with the same problems men have always faced in business, but also with problems relating to their home life, their married life, and of course their sexual life. Irene, with a taste of power on the job, with the realization that she was capable of making wise decisions, was no longer able to play a passive role in her marriage. Her problem with power was not how to use it at work, but how to get it at home.

But most women run into problems with the use of power on the job. This can be deep-rooted problem for a woman who has grown up in a society that has assigned to her a nurturing role. One woman who entered the business world paid what she considered a terrible price.

"I've been in the cosmetics industry all my adult life," Sarah told me. "I started modeling makeup when I was just a kid, and then I took a course in advertising. I was hired as copywriter by a big outfit. I won't bore you with my climb up the corporate ladder as a woman, but I used everything I had, my looks as well as my ability. I really know the field, and eventually I got the break I wanted. I was working on the managerial level for one of the bigger cosmetic outfits, and I was put in charge of their eastern branch. The branch was in big trouble, and my orders were to 'turn it around'."

"I can tell you, it was a break, but it shook me up. I was in my early forties, a woman in a very competitive field. I knew all the power games men play, and while I could play them too, they scared the hell out of me. I spent three weeks studying that eastern branch without going near it. My conclusion was that it was a disaster area and something had to be done quickly to save it. It had been mismanaged from the ground up. In fact, I even wondered if they hadn't given the job to me because it was so hopeless and they'd get a kick out of seeing a woman fall on her face. Perhaps that's a bit paranoid, but you get that way when you're a woman in business."

"Well, once I knew what had to be done, the big problem was did I have the power to do it? I had *carte blanche* from the higher-ups, but what I needed was the complete cooperation of the managers at the new plant. Where would I get the power to command that?

"I felt that desperate situations call for desperate measures. I called the branch and told them I would arrive in three hours. I had spent close to a thousand dollars on clothes for that meeting, including the rental of a fabulous mink coat. I don't think a Hollywood costume designer could have done a better job of outfitting me and I worked out a complete scenario. I arrived in a limousine with five assistants, two of the most efficient and best-looking secretaries, and three men, two in their thirties and one in his fifties, an athletic, white-haired type. Believe me, I orchestrated the whole thing."

"I immediately called a meeting of the ten top

managers of the branch. I had spent a week studying their performance records, everything about them. There were three rotten apples in the barrel, and my first step was to fire all three and tell them I wanted them out of the building by five. Then I laid out exactly what was wrong with the branch and what I intended to do. Then, very deliberately, I told them that anyone, *anyone* I caught standing in my way would not only be fired, but I would personally guarantee that he would never work in the industry again. Then I stood up and told them my secretaries would schedule meetings with each of them, starting at 7:00 A.M. tomorrow. After that I took my mink and stalked out, my three male assistants following me very smartly.''

"I tell you, that was a rough scenario to stick to, but I did. In the limousine, going home that afternoon, I thought I'd come apart at the seams. But you know, it worked. I had that company turned around in six months, and every one of those managers cooperated with me right down the line. I had set up a power situation based on three factors. One, appearance. I came in there looking and smelling like success. The limousine, the mink, my assistants, the secretaries—they all created an aura of power. Two, I had the power of surprise. I caught them off guard, giving them only a few hour's warning of my arrival, and immediately fired the troublemakers. And, three, I had done my homework. They all knew who the troublemakers were, and they were shook up because I knew too. It all helped, along with my threat to fire anyone who opposed me. A few words in the right places—what I had going for me was know-how. I knew what had to be done. I'd studied the situation, and I knew the business, and I had the authority to back up anything I did. I showed that authority immediately by firing the three men."

"It worked," I agreed, "but you said that you paid a terrible price. What was it?"

Sarah looked at me bleakly. "I overheard some of them talking about me some weeks later. One of them was a man I liked who was damned good at his job. I really thought he understood and respected me and what I had done, but I heard him call me a frigid bitch. His friend laughed and wondered whom I'd slept with to get the job." She shook her head slowly. "If a man had wielded power like that, he'd be admired. But a woman . . ."

What Sarah was saying in effect is that our perception of power changes depending on whether it is used by a man or a woman. We see a ruthless act of power by a man as a sign of toughness, strength, competence and certainty. Such an act, we concede, is masculine.

In a woman, the same act is somehow out of character. We see it as bitchy, cold, threatening, unwomanly, castrating. Our society has set up certain roles for women to play, and even the women themselves feel uncomfortable when they step outside of those roles. It's a rare woman who can handle power as competently as a man and still feel at ease with herself.

You Scratch My Back—I'll Scratch Yours

Sarah's method of exerting power is a valid one in the business world, but there are other equally valid methods that may be just as successful and perhaps more comfortable for women. Gwen has a job as editor-in-chief of a very popular "ladies" magazine, and she manages a staff of over a hundred men and women.

"The secretaries and typists are no problem," Gwen told me. "They're sensible and good workers. I treat them fairly, and they do a good job. But the editors and writers are another story. It takes a Machiavelli to keep them in line."

"How do you do it?" I asked, recalling Sarah's hard-line treatment. Gwen is nothing like Sarah. She's a big woman, physically and emotionally, outgoing and friendly.

"How do I do it? It's a variation of the old scratch-my-back-I'll-scratch-yours game. Look, I'm known in the industry for the loyalty of the people under me. A little while ago a popular man's magazine tried to lure away Tom, one of my top editors. They told him, 'Hey, you shouldn't be working for a woman. Come on over to us and you can have all these goodies.' You know what Tom told them? And I got this from one of their editors, not from Tom. He told them, 'I'd do anything Gwen wanted. I know she doesn't want me to leave.' Now that's what I call loyalty. And with loyalty like that I've got power."

"How do you get loyalty like that?"

"With Tom is wasn't any one thing. I see him as a human being, not as a worker. I treat him as a friend. When his mother died last fall, I went to the funeral. Partly because I cared, and also because I wanted him to know I cared. When his wife was sick, I made him take a week off, and I sent flowers. I never forget his anniversary, and I keep tabs on his family when he travels. I make sure they're all right. Oh hell, I act like a mother hen. I know all my staff by name. The point is, I develop true friendship with all of them, and friendships like that carry certain obligations. Their obligation to me is loyalty."

"That sounds manipulative," I said.

She looked at me somberly. "Does it? Well, I have news for you. All power is manipulative, all managerial power. The bottom line is the perception of the person who's being manipulated. If he sees the manipulation as friendship, it will work. I love my job, and though it may not sound sincere to you, I love the people who work for me. If I don't, I get rid of them. I've got a good loyal staff because I'm loyal to them!"

That was Gwen's way of handling power, and it is certainly an effective way, a method used by men as well as women. It is also, incidentally, a method that women find very comfortable. In interviewing dozens of women in managerial positions, I found many more using Gwen's techniques than Sarah's. They instilled a sense of obligation in their subordinates in order to arouse a sense of loyalty.

The Expert Technique

Another method of gaining power, used by both men and women, but one that women are either more comfortable with, or, as often happens, are forced into, is the *expert technique*. When someone is recognized as an expert in his field he has enough power to manage others.

"I'm head of the psychiatric department in my

hospital," Anne told me, "and it hasn't been easy, particularly since three quarters of the doctors under me are men. Add to that the fact that physically I don't look authoritative."

That was an understatement. Physically Anne looks like a competitor for the role of one of Charlie's Angels. Delicate, with shoulder-length blond hair and large blue eyes, very pretty and very feminine, she looks like the epitome of the "dumb blonde." And you expect her to be that, or at least filled with the old feminine wiles. In actual fact, Anne is a level-headed and intelligent research worker. She also knows how to run a department. "But without power I could never do it," she admitted.

"How did you get the power?" I asked.

"By proving to everyone in my department, and in the entire hospital for that matter, that I am thoroughly competent. To do that I have to be successful in almost every case I handle, and I have to be better than the other doctors."

"How can you be?"

"I can," she smiled, "if I select the cases I treat in the hospital setting. I only treat patients I am sure I can help. In my private practice it's a different story. As a matter of fact, to compensate, I tend to treat more difficult cases than most psychiatrists do. But here, in the hospital, I have a reputation for success. Another thing, I publish more than anyone else, and I attend more seminars and psychiatric meetings, and here's a tip to anyone who wants to improve their reputation. At all of these meetings I keep my mouth shut if the discussion is one I'm not *very* familiar with. But I speak up very forcibly if it is something I know for certain. You've no idea how that helps a reputation!''

Power by Identification

In an article in the Harvard Business Review, John P. Kotter, associate professor of business administration at the Harvard Business School, reported on a study of thirty-six business organizations, large and small, public and private, manufacturing and service. Interviewing three-hundred-fifty managers, Professor Kotter listed the above three management techniques as effective male methods of obtaining power. Another method, according to him, is identification. When a subordinate finds a manager an "ideal" person, he will identify with him. For this kind of identification the trappings of power are important—the proper clothes, the proper appearance, the proper attitude. But rather than change his image to gain this identification, many managers will hire only people who can achieve the identification easily, sometimes people of the same ethnic group, the same religious race, or even people with similar backgrounds. In one office, managed by a woman, she achieved this identification by hiring only women in every capacity.

Women like Laura, Gwen and Anne are close to the top of their profession, but they are a rarity. In general women don't reach the upper echelons of power. At the top of the corporate ladder, men outnumber women 600 to 1, and most of the few women who are in power have inherited or married the power. They are either the daughters of wealthy fathers or the wives of wealthy men. As we go down the corporate ladder, the percentage of women in power increases.

Most women in business or the professions work at a submanagerial level, and most are responsible for men. How then does a woman who clocks in at the secretary or bookkeeper level go about getting power? Traditionally, in society, women have gained their power through men. The wife acquires the social and financially powerful mantle of her husband. If a woman wants power, she searches for a marriage that will give it to her. She selects a husband with either great promise or with great power.

In the business world, the same procedures operate. I talked to Millie who is executive secetary to the president of a small drug company. Millie had joined the firm fifteen years ago in the packaging department. She was a friendly, hard-working woman who had promptly set about bettering herself. She went to night school and learned secretarial skills, then talked personnel into giving her a chance in the typist's pool. From there she worked her way up in the organization.

"What I always aimed for was becoming secretary to the most important man in the company," she admitted. "I knew that was the way to get ahead."

"Did you ever think of switching over to any other department?" I asked, "Sales or advertising? Wouldn't there have been better opportunities there?"

"As a secretary? Oh no."

"No, I mean as a detail man—or detail woman—or as a copywriter."

She laughed at my naïveté. "You've got to be kidding. A woman doesn't stand a chance in sales or advertising, not unless she's made it in some other outfit. They don't train women on the job. No, the best I could do was in secretarial work, and I've done damned well there."

In a way, she had. Millie was good, a hard worker, intelligent and aggressive, but the only way she could get power in her organization was to attach herself to a powerful man. Had she been a man with the same ability there would have been many opportunities open to her, including the possibility of rising into the corporate power structure of the organization.

Hilda, a co-worker of Millie, is also eager for power. She too is an executive secretary, but her technique for obtaining power is to make herself indispensable to her boss. She has taken over not only all of his office responsibilities, but a good deal of his personal responsibilities as well. She keeps track of family birthdays, buys presents and send them out in his name, remembers anniversaries and chooses gifts for him, and even takes over some of his wife's social duties. When her boss's wife headed a local charity, Hilda was the one who planned the fundraising campaign and did all the paper work at home in her free time.

"Don't you resent it?" I asked her.

She shook her head. "No, I love it. They both appreciate what I do for them, and to tell you the truth, I don't know how they'd get along without me. Between restaurant reservations and theatre tickets, they're practically helpless."

They are, in fact, as helpless as Hilda has contrived to make them, and she is as powerful as they are helpless.

The Impotent Tycoon

When I began investigating "woman power," I was constantly told that sex was one of the prime ways that woman attained power in the business world—told this, I must add, by men. "Sleeping her way up the corporate ladder" was a constant phrase used to describe a woman who had made it. But I've come to the conclusion that sex in business is used to put women down, much the way it was used by the man Sarah overheard. What seems to be more common in sexual politics is that if a woman worker enters into an affair with her boss, she usually suffers for it. When the affair breaks up, the odds are that she will prove an embarrassment and lose her job.

It is much more common for the man in a business situation to try to use his power to force a sexual encounter. The woman who refuses finds her job at risk. If there is an advantage of sexual bartering in business, it is a dubious one, and it lasts only as long as the sexual encounter. Afterwards the woman becomes an embarrassment, and somehow or other she must be gotten out of the way. The power in the situation lies with the man, rarely if ever, outside of some lurid novels, with the woman.

Sex, on the other hand, can be an important asset to male power. The man who holds a powerful position is respected for any sexual encounter he may have. His power is enhanced by seduction, and the more beautiful and "expensive" the woman he seduces, the greater the respect accorded to him. This is so true that often men, happy in their married situation, will still go after expensive mistresses simply for the power factor.

Dr. Offit, talking to me about power and businessmen in a sexual situation, cited the example of a very powerful middle-aged man she had treated. "He ran a large manufacturing business with an iron hand. You could really classify him as an old fashioned tycoon. All the power of the company was channeled through him. He made the most far-reaching decisions and carried a tremendous load of responsibility. And he had all the trappings of power—a beautiful home in the suburbs, and apartment in town, a chauffered limousine in addition to his Rolls-Royce. He had a warm, retiring wife who devoted herself to the home and children—and an exquisitely beautiful mistress he had set up in a very classy downtown apartment."

"It sounds," I said dubiously, "like the plot for a four-part television mini-series."

"Doesn't it? But the curious thing about this tycoon was that he had no sex with his mistress. As a matter of fact, he couldn't. He was impotent with her."

"How strange. I could understand the set-up if he was impotant with his wife."

"But that's just it. He wasn't. To the contrary, he had a very good sexual relationship with his wife. He loved her and he loved his children. He spent all the time he could with his family."

"It doesn't add up. Why the mistress?"

"Ah, why the limousine and the Rolls? They are trappings of power, signs of success—and so is a beautiful, talented mistress."

"Are you telling me he had a mistress simply for appearance's sake?"

116

"That's exactly what I'm telling you. It was a symbol to show the rest of the world just how powerful he was."

"And they both stood for it, his mistress and his wife?"

"Why not? The mistress was no threat to his wife. She understood exactly what the mistress stood for. She had her husband and all the prestige that went with him, and she had a good sexual life with him. As for the mistress, she had everything she wanted. He was a generous man and she wasn't inconvenienced by his sexual desires. To a woman like that, sex would be an inconvenience. No, the three of them were very content with the arrangement."

"Yes, I can see that, but I find it hard to understand why he was impotent with his mistress."

"Just because she was so expensive, so beautiful. He saw her as something above him, something he wasn't worthy of."

"Tell me—tycoons, men like that, men with a great deal of power—don't they also have a powerful sex drive? I mean, I would think they'd have as much of a sexual need as they have a need for power? At least, they always seem to especially in fiction."

"But fiction is wrong. I've treated many, many men like that, and it's a funny thing with them. They tend to be homebodies. In bed, as in all domestic areas, their women have the power. Their women are the bosses. On a sexual level, the men don't feel in charge."

"Why?"

"Because sexuality isn't their domain. Business is their domain, and so is public appearances.

Home is their wife's domain, home, and the bed, and sex."

"Is this a reason why a successful businessman might go to someone like a call girl?"

Dr. Offit nodded. "Yes. She's not threatening, not a mother. But you know, impotence is frequent in men like that. In my experience, the more social and financial power a man has, the greater the risk of impotence. On the other hand, the quiet, non-aggressive men who aren't interested in power are generally much more secure sexually.

"A woman I was treating was married to one of those typical, high-pressured executives who had a tremendous amount of power on the job. As a lover he was a terrible disappointment to her, and eventually they separated.

"After the divorce she met a young high school teacher and had an affair with him and then married him. He was gentle, easy-going, happy in his job and completely disinterested in power, and she found that sexually he was a wonderful lover. He seemed to have no questions about his manhood, and he functioned as a man. Her first husband had always been concerned with his masculinity, and that was behind his drive for power—and also behind the fact that he was a lousy lover."

The Fear of Power

Can we equate the drive for power with an inner insecurity, a fear of not being strong enough? Can we say that the man who has a drive to secure power is also a man constantly afraid that he hasn't the ability to get power? By the same reasoning, is the man who is disinterested in power a man who has enough inner strength, who doesn't need power to shore up his masculinity?

I talked this over with a professor of psychiatry at one of our large midwestern universities. "There is some truth to that," he agreed, "but there is also too much simplification. True, some men turn to power in order to cover up their own inadequacies, and many men who are comfortable with their masculinity don't need power. But you must add, many men who avoid power have a fear of it."

"A fear of power?" I asked. "For what reason?"

He spread his hands. "Usually it's a family thing. I call it the baby-in-the-family syndrome. A youngest child will develop a fear of power if his older brothers and sisters were very powerful. They'll inhibit his ability to be powerful as a child, and this inhibition will spread to later life. Such an inhibition, or fear, comes from being the victim of power. Such a victim will also develop a fear of his own power because, as a child, whenever he used power he was put down by his older siblings.

"As a grown man, this younger son will hesitate about getting into a power situation, and he may, indeed, grow up to be very ineffective. As he grows older, he will usually develop an inner conflict between wanting power and fearing it, and yet he may be very afraid not to have it. He'll want to be on his own, out of any organization or job where power plays go on. Such a man would tend to drop out of jobs whenever a power problem entered."

"But how does that relate to the man I described, the gentle, easy-going man distinterested in power?"

119

"Ah, but what causes his disinterest? Is it a genuine indifference, or is it a fear of power?"

"But if his disinterest in power makes him a happy man, does it really matter?"

"No, I suppose not, any more than it matters that the power-driven man may be very happy with the power he gets. And if he is, does it matter that he went after that power because of some basic insecurity? No, the motives for power are often too obscure to dig up. What is important is how we handle the power, whether we are happy with it or unhappy. If it makes us unhappy we should avoid it, and if it makes us happy we should go after it. There's a simplification for you."

"Do women suffer from the same fear of power?" I asked him.

"Much more so than men. A woman doesn't have to be the youngest child to have powerful others in the family. A younger brother can be more powerful, and her father is always an example of power she shouldn't challenge. Inevitably there is some fear of power in most women. Check out some working women and you'll see."

I did indeed "see" once I followed his advice. In almost all work situations, it's a rarity to find women supervising men, and if they do, they are expected to use their power in a nurturing manner. One executive woman told me, "I supervise six men, and I have their respect because I know the job better than any of them. But still, when I have to criticize something they've done, I phrase my criticism very carefully. It's always, 'I think *we've* goofed on this one, boys,' never 'I think *you've* goofed.' They really couldn't take that. All in all, I can't even give a definite command to them if I want to keep things going well, and I do want that for my own benefit. I want my department to function smoothly. So I coax, suggest and even involve myself in the mistake to appear unaggressive."

This executive has learned that when women show power they are generally punished in some way. The men will inevitably get back at them even if they do so by making enough of a poor showing to endanger her supervision. "I usually have to hide my talents," she told me. "I really can't let them see that I'm as good or better than they are—even though I am!"

She is afraid of power because a woman showing her power in a male-dominated world runs a dangerous risk. "Nor is it any better when you deal with other women," she hastened to add. "They too find it hard to trust another woman with more power than they have, or then women usually have. I seem to be a threat to them just because I've made it. If one woman makes it in an outfit, they feel no other ever will."

This woman's experience is not unique. In the sciences and in politics as well as in business, women have been discouraged by their teachers and colleagues, shut out of jobs, denied a political party's support and backing, and in general made to feel that holding power was unwomanly and wrong.

First their fathers and brothers, then the world, helps to instill a fear of power in them. And yet, once they overcame this fear and the conditions that cause it, women have as great a need for power, whether it's creative or manipulative, as men do.

In dealing with power, women face not only the

problem of fear, but also one of guilt. They go hand in hand. In our society, the woman who succeeds in achieving power is treated as if, in some way, she has lost a basic quality. While boys and men are taught to equate power with masculinity, girls and women are taught to equate it with a lack of feminity. All of our stories, our literature, our deepest folklore, link women to passivity, to compliance. Femininity is defined as becoming an appendage to men, deferring to them on all levels, at home and at work.

I know of two sisters, very close in age, who chose two different paths in llife. Greta, the youngest, made a "good" marriage and had two children. Her husband had a small business and they were quite comfortable.

Her sister, Elsie, wanted more out of life than domesticity. She went through law school, joined a well known law firm and achieved a great deal of prominence when she successfully defended a large corporation accused of polluting the environment.

Yet, in a recent visit home, Elsie told me that after half a day she felt no sense of triumph or achievement.

"There I was, a successful lawyer in a traditionally male field, and I had just pulled off a major coup. I expected congratulations, and do you know what my mother said? 'Now when are you going to meet a nice man and settle down?' My father put his arm around me and told my mother, 'Now don't you worry. Elsie is smart. Why do you think she entered a profession with so many men? She'll find someone soon.' And there you have it. My sister Greta was the success. She had the symbols of feminine power, a husband and kids! Me, all I had was a terrific job, a promising future and work I loved doing. To them it was all worthless!''

5

THE BODY LANGUAGE OF POWER

A Ride on the New York Subways

Recently, I had to take a long subway ride in New York City and the car, ugly with graffiti, promised a very depressing half hour. Looking around the car at the bored or preoccupied riders, I was suddenly brought up short by the challenging stare of a young man in his early twenties.

I sat up a bit straighter, pleased that the ride wouldn't be a total waste of time. Here was a genuine starer and a chance for me to make some first-hand observations. I broke eye contact at once. I wasn't interested in my own reactions to staring. I wanted the reactions of the other passengers.

I glanced back at the starer surreptitiously, without making eye contact, and I noticed a fleeting quirk of the lips, a touch of contempt at my easy defeat. I was worth nothing as an opponent. He glanced over the other passengers, and his eyes caught those of a young woman. Aha, a contest! But again it was too easy a victory. The woman blushed, embarrassed, and broke off contact quickly to pretend interest in an advertisement above the seats. A nervous young man was next, but he only lasted a few seconds. Then an old lady. She frowned in annoyance and began to go through her purse, another avoidance technique. One by one the weaker sisters and brothers were stared down, and the starer seemed to gain a little more power with each defeat.

Then he met his match. A tough-looking, bearded youth got on at the next stop, sat down and, undaunted, locked eyes with the challenger. This was going to be no easy battle. The two stared at each other with unblinking intensity for three stops. Then, with a satisfied smile, the challenger stood up. This was his stop. The contest was a draw. The challenged one watched him go with an equally satisfied smile and a little nod of the head, which was returned. Surprised, I thought, those two like each other!

I understood the easy victories. People who are reluctant to handle power, or who tend to be passive and let others dominate them, will almost always walk away from a staring contest. They dislike starers. But I was puzzled by the two starers smiling at each other. Surely they had been in conflict only a few seconds before.

The answer came a few days later when I read through the report of a study by Dr. Walter James Lawless. He had set up a number of "laboratory staring situations" between people who were very dominant and some who were quite shy. His findings agreed with those I had experienced on the subway car, and he also explained the puzzling attraction of the two very dominant starers. People like that, he concluded, people who initiate challenging power games such as staring another person down see a potential ally in someone who resists them. The strong attract the strong as much as they repel the weak. Power, it seems, attracts power.

When I described the subway staring episode to a psychologist friend of mine, he nodded knowingly. "But you mustn't think that this kind of arrogant staring is a healthy expression of power."

"What do you mean?" I asked.

"I mean," he said slowly, "it's a very ugly invasion of privacy. Staring is a power play, yes. The strong can stare at the weak, but for the weak it's a humiliating experience. You told me the first girl he stared at blushed and was embarrassed. This is a common reaction in a woman to the bold stare of a man. A stare says, "You are an object, not a person." We stare at animals in zoos, but we avoid staring at other people. Your subway starer borders on the pathological. I myself would refuse to play power games with someone like that. He could easily become violent."

I was reminded of his words a few days later. I was in a small cocktail lounge waiting for my wife, and I looked around, surprised at the number of single women before I realized that we had evidently picked an active singles bar to meet in.

At that point a young, good-looking man entered. He paused in the entrance, aware of the quick interest his arrival had aroused. I saw him scan the room, catching the eyes of the young women, one by one. Each one, after a quick glance, broke eye contact, except for one young woman who returned his look with a level glance for a shade beyond the accepted length of time. It wouldn't qualify as a stare, but it was certainly longer than the quick instances of eye contact the other women permitted.

The young man completed his sweep around the room, hesitated only a few minutes at the bar to get a drink, then approached the woman who had returned his glance. There were smiles exchanged, a few words, and then he sat down next to her with his drink.

A good beginning, I decided. He had used eye contact to single out the one young woman interested enough to be picked up, and now they were getting along just fine.

Unlike the rude starer in the subway, this man used eye contact to determine which of the women in the crowd would be likely to accept his overtures. There was no question of his own power in the situation. It takes a good deal of aggression to initiate this sort of game—it also takes aggression to accept the challenge.

There is a *moral looking-time* for every situation. In a crowded elevator it is no time at all. You refuse to catch anyone's eye. You look at the floor numbers, at the door, anywhere but at your fellow passengers.

The moral looking-time is a bit longer in a bus or subway train, and longer still in a cocktail lounge. The young man I watched tried to violate that time with each woman who caught his eye. When one woman allowed him to do it, he knew she was receptive. She would at least talk to him if he approached her. It was a quick way to separate the disinterested from the interested.

"I found out that violating the moral looking-time can often separate the more powerful men from the weaker," a director of personnel of a Dallas-based oil company told me. "I was given an unusual assignment some months ago. My supervisor told me that the company was looking for a number of aggressive men, men who could play a dominant role in a new foreign development project. 'You've got to find some way of cutting through the resumes,' he told me. 'Some technique during the interviews to use to discover who are the very dominant men.' "

"It took me a little while, but I found just that technique. Normally, I dislike prolonged eye contact. Like most people, I'm comfortable with a five or six-second 'fix,' and then I like to breack contact. In the interviews I set up for the new positions, I broke my own rules and forced myself to hold eye contact as long as the other person let me. It was an instant success with separating the wheat from the chaff. Most people squirmed uncomfortably, broke eye contact very quickly and seemed thrown off-base by my insistent stare.

"But every once in a while I'd meet a candidate whose eyes seemed to light up as he took the challenge, who returned my stare squarely, firmly and comfortably a few seconds longer than the moral looking-time and who, oddly enough, seemed to have a close rapport with me afterwards, as if that little 'game' had created a closeness between us. I'd know then that I had found one of the men the company needed, a man aggressive enough to be comfortable with power."

A Question of Feedback

The ability to make and hold extended eye contact is one indication of a powerful personality. Eye contact is a part of body language, the most important part in terms of communication. Body language is what we say with our bodies, over and above what we say with our voices. Sometimes body language amplifies the spoken word, emphasizes or exaggerates it, and sometimes it contradicts it. We can lie very easily with our words, but since body language is unconscious, it is much more difficult to use it to lie. We may tell someone we love him when we don't, and often our heads will unconsciously move from side to side signaling "no" and giving the lie to our statement.

It is just this unconscious element of body language that we should consider in terms of power. The ability not only to be comfortable in a staring situation, but also to return the stare and feel an identification with the starer can be interpreted in terms of body language.

However, the average person responds to a "rude" stare with annoyance or anger. It signals aggression. To enjoy such a stare is a sign of a very powerful personality, a desire to meet an aggressor halfway and enjoy the encounter.

It is possible to "fake" this aggressive stare, but it is not possible to fake our reaction. Unless we are equally aggressive, we will feel uncomfortable and uneasy in a staring situation. It does no good to assume the trappings of power, to conduct yourself in a powerful fashion, unless there is a feeling of true power within you. It is that feeling of power that must be developed before you can resort to any of the games of power.

The problem, then, is how do we develop this inner sense of power? Is there anything we can do to strengthen our inner selves?

Dr. Alexander Lowen, in his writings, gives us a number of clues to the answer. He describes case after case where patients came to him with troubled personalities reflected in troubled bodies. A body which did not function up to its full potential indicated to Lowen a pattern of behavior which also fell below its full potential.

I discussed this concept with an athletic coach in a small western college. Nils had had over fifteen years of coaching experience on the college level. "You must understand," he told me one day while we watched a group of young men on the football field, "that there is a feedback process at work in people. I agree with what you've told me about Dr. Lowen's work, but I'll take it a step beyond. I can cite you example after example of poor students—poor in terms of their ability to study, concentrate and absorb knowledge—who began to work out in one sport or another and after two or three weeks suddenly became aware of a change in their mental attitude."

"What kind of a change?"

"Everything picked up for them. They were able to study, able to concentrate in class, they became better students."

"That puzzles me a little," I said. "Wouldn't you think the opposite would be true, that the workout in sports would take too much out of them, exhaust them?"

Nils put a hand on my shoulder, stood up and blew his whistle. "I'll be right back," he said. "Wait for me." He trotted out on the field to settle some dispute, then hurried back. "The funny thing is," he said, sitting down beside me, "working out like this doesn't exhaust young men—or old men—for that matter. Hell, I run. I've been doing it for years, four or five miles a morning before breakfast. Now, on the days I run, I feel great, physically and mentally alert. If I have to skip my running for, say, bad weather, I just don't feel right for that day. It's the same with these kids. Make them active, and their bodies change. They stand a little straighter, begin to breathe more deeply, and suddenly they're alive, alert—I can't begin to tell you how important I think workouts are, and not just because it's my field." He chewed his lower lip for a minute. "There's another thing—posture. You change the way a man walks, get him to walk straighter, taller, and you change something inside him. I swear you do."

Some months later I was having lunch with a plain-clothes detective from the New York City Police Department. We had been discussing methods of discouraging criminals, and I brought up the body language feedback theory, citing Nils' experience. "Have you found anything like that with your police?" I asked.

"Yes, but before I go into that, you asked me about crime and victims a little while ago, and I want to mention one thing. There are ways of cutting down on your chances of becoming a victim, and one is by your body language. Walk like a victim, and you increase your chances of becoming one. Walk with an erect, non-nonsense gait, walk tough, and you decrease your chances of being mugged or attacked. No mugger likes to tangle with someone who'll give him trouble. Walk as if you won't be a pushover and you're a bit safer."

"Now you asked about police, and it's true. We teach them body language, how to stand, how to

131

walk, how to carry themselves in all kinds of situations, and I've found that there is a definite feedback. The taller they stand, the taller they feel—the more powerful their movements, the more powerful they become. Oh, it doesn't happen overnight, but it's a definite, continuing process. Still, all this shouldn't come as a big surprise to you."

"Why shouldn't it?"

"You were in the army. Don't you remember being taught to walk and stand a certain way? That was how you made a soldier, by shaping the outside of the man, by teaching him to walk erect, to march to a beat, to be crisp and military. Eventually he began to feel like a soldier inside—at least most of us did."

I had to agree, and I found the idea of feedback confirmed by many psychologists, psychiatrists and psychoanalysts. A New York City analyst told me, "There is such a strong correlation between body language and mood that I can diagnose most of my patients before they open their mouths simply by the way they sit and stand and move."

"What I am after," I told him, "is the possibility of feedback. Do you change if you change your body language?"

"It's a continuing circle, or spiral, really," he explained. "If you become a bit more aggressive in your body language, for example, then there is a feedback to your personality, and you feel more aggressive. In turn, this aggressive feeling allows you to move more aggressively, and in turn that changes your inner self a bit more."

"But if that's so, why doesn't everyone with a touch of aggression go into that spiral and become increasingly more aggressive?"

132

"It's a process that must be fueled by a constant desire to change. As long as you genuinely wish to make yourself more aggressive, the spiral works.

"What we are talking about," he went on, "is the strengthening of the inner self, the ego. To be aggressive, and I mean aggressive in a positive way, to be assertive and powerful, you must have an inner self that is equally strong and powerful. Our body language not only reflects our inner self; it also influences it in a classic feedback mechanism.

"Eye contact is a basic body language signal, and I use it on my depressed patients. Depression signals itself by, among other things, an avoidance of eye contact. To change them, I get my patients to attempt eye contact, small doses of it at first and in non-threatening situations."

"What is a non-threatening situation?"

"An encounter with someone they knew or love, or with someone who is below them in status. I get them to try meeting the eye of a supermarket clerk, a child, a ticket seller at a theatre or a waiter in a restaurant—simple eye contact. I don't let them try to hold eye contact; simply making it is enough. If they can do that successfully, it's a first step in strengthening the self."

It is also a first step towards power, I discovered. The depressed person is one with very little power, even though not all powerless people are depressed. But whether you take that first step to get out of depression, or to move towards power, the technique is the same. You start to strengthen your body language, and this strengthening in turn exerts a feedback. It strengthens your personality.

If we are to strengthen our body language, we must first understand just how body language relates to power. Eye contact is one important element that does affect power. How we manage space is another. Each of us, no matter what our power needs, has a sense of territory, a feeling that certain areas are our own. Sometimes it is as simple as where we sit at our dining room table, or it may be a bit more complex. A wife will think of the kitchen as "my kitchen" and may resent not only her husband coming into it, but any friend who wants to help her. The kitchen is her territory, just as the den may be her husband's. He may also have his favorite chair and be troubled if anyone else sits in it. I know a married couple who have carried this so far that they have "his" and "hers" bathrooms.

In church we have our favorite pews, our territory, just as in the schoolroom a student will select one particular seat and sit there at each session. In the movie *A Touch of Class,* a divorced American, played by George Segal, tries to get an Englishwoman, played by Glenda Jackson, into bed. When he finally does, the moment before he starts to make love, he sits up and asks, "Would you mind changing sides?"

For many of us, our sense of territory extends this far, to one particular side of the bed. We just aren't comfortable sleeping or making love on either side of a double bed.

On a more intimate level, our sense of territoriality is expressed in private body space. Each of us carries around a bubble of privacy, much like an astronaut's helmet. The size of the bubble varies from culture to culture. In the Arab world it is usually only six inches. In our culture it is a full two feet. How we manage that space can be a power play, sometimes a completely unconscious one. Recently, an American oil company executive, back from Saudi Arabia, told how this disparity in personal space had almost spoiled an important oil deal.

"I met with an Arab representative of OPEC to discuss the final phrases of our agreement, and as we talked he moved in to what was his comfortable social distance, a half foot away. At the time I didn't realize it, I was pretty new in the Middle East, and I moved back to my comfortable distance, two feet. He hesitated, frowned a bit, and moved closer to me. I started to step back, and then I caught the eye of my assistant. He glared at me and shook his head, and thank heaven I caught on. I stayed put and we concluded the deal in what, to me, was the most strained and uncomfortable position I've ever been in.

"But my assistant, a native Saudi, explained that to the OPEC man, my moving back to two feet was something of an insult, as if to say, 'I don't want to be this close. You offend me.' "

In our own culture, moving in on someone else's private space can be a troubling power play. If someone comes too close, we feel threatened, defenseless and exposed. The exception, of course, is when someone we love—our wife, lover, child, parent or close friend—violates that private space. Then it doesn't seem like a violation or an intrusion. It becomes a simple declaration of affection, or even of love.

In a business situation, an executive may violate

135

a subordinate's zone of privacy by looming over his desk. It becomes an obnoxious power play. But another type of violation, an arm around the shoulder at a crucial moment, can be a show of affection and warmth. At the wrong moment, it can arouse an uneasy feeling.

Violating one's territory can be an expression of power, even if the violator is not in a powerful position or is not a powerful person. I recall an incident on a city bus, where a rather frail old lady bent over a seated man engrossed in a newspaper. She said nothing, but though the aisle was relatively empty, she chose this particular space to intrude.

The seated reader noticed her and tried to ignore her. He was comfortable where he was and evidently had a long ride ahead, but he became increasingly more uncomfortable, shifted around, tried to avoid her eyes and finally, with a sigh of exasperation, folded his newspaper and stood up. With a sweet little smile, the old woman slipped expertly into his seat, elbowing out another woman who had just come down the aisle. Small and frail as she was, she had perfected a very neat little power play.

Of course you needn't be weak to indulge in these unpleasant little power games. I have been in many crowded buses where husky young men sprawled across more than one seat, daring any other passenger to compete for equal seating. Other young men will keep to one seat, but will spread their arms along the back of the seat on either side. You can either ask them to remove their arms, or sit and hope that they will. They usually do move away because this type of power game is part bluff, part intimidation.

Young men and older adolescents are very attracted to this type of flexing of their power muscles. Often it's a testing out of a new found strength, but when the adolescents come from poverty areas, from deprived backgrounds, another factor can enter the game. Poverty is no respecter of power. On the contrary, it deprives young people of power. It is this sense of being powerless that often causes such young people to indulge in so many territorial power games, sprawling over seats in a crowded bus, deliberately blocking doorways and passages, jostling and pushing in crowds—all these gambits are attempts to gain a little extra power.

Building Personal Power

Once we link the invasion of personal space with power, we arrive at the next step. Is there some way to increase your own inner sense of power through invading someone else's space? Power and aggression are closely linked, and increasing your aggression will increase your sense of power. Again, as with eye contact, we must start with small, non-threatening situations.

I have mentioned buses a number of times, and they are, for many reasons, perfect testing grounds for power plays, especially those buses with a row of seats along either side and an aisle down the middle. If you ever have the opportunity to get onto a bus like that when it is almost empty, watch the way the seats fill up. There is an unspoken rule among people that they will not sit next to anyone if they can help it.

Given all this empty space, the bus will fill up in a predictable way, with each passenger leaving an empty seat on either side of him as he sits. It is only when the bus gets so full that it becomes impossible to leave an empty seat between you and your neighbor, that these extra seats start to fill up and people will sit alongside someone else. Here we have the elements of a fine exercise in power development for the shy person. Let him board a very empty bus and deliberately sit next to someone without leaving a seat in between!

If you do try this ploy, however, be sure to pick your own sex. In an empty bus, the man who sits next to a woman is making a sexual as well as a power statement.

Another exercise in territorial power development is to use an aggressive manner when you enter the office of someone in authority. There are many ways of entering an office. You can knock, wait for someone to call out "Come in" and then open the door and poke your head in. This the most timid approach, the one that indicates the least internal power. If that's your regular approach, it may mean you're in trouble.

The most aggressive entrance is made without knocking. You open the door and walk in and up to the desk of whoever's office it is. Then loom over him as you talk.

In between these two, there are a wide range of techniques. You can knock and enter without waiting to be asked in, knock and walk in and up to the desk, enter without knocking but stand near the door, or enter without knocking and come right up to the desk.

You can judge your own sense of inner power by

deciding which approach seems most comfortable to you. As you rise up the scale of aggressive entrances, your own power potential increases. If you are low on the scale, deliberately try a more aggressive entrance, one up the ladder. Once you get used to that and feel comfortable with it (a sign the feedback is working) go on to the next aggressive entrance.

Eye contact and territoriality are two parts of body language that are involved with power. A third important part is body movement. The psychiatrist who told me he could diagnose depression from his patient's body language, was referring, in part, to the way his patient moved. In terms of movement, there is a body language of depression just as there is one of power.

"I can tell," a maitre' d in an expensive restaurant told me, "just how much a customer is worth financially by the way he walks. For that matter, I can even tell what kind of a tip he'll leave. Your rich or powerful man just walks differently."

He was right. The posture of a powerful man is a bit straighter. There is an assurance to the way he carries himself. He walks lightly and with great self-confidence, often with a touch of arrogance.

But the body language of power goes beyond walking. It is comprised of all the movements of the body. A powerful person will project his power with his hand movements. There is no hesitation or uncertainty in them. There is even power when he doesn't move. Some people are comfortable remaining quiet while others move around them. There is power in solidity just as there is in slow, deliberate movement.

In attempting to improve your own body movement, you must first see yourself objectively, as others do. Do you walk decisively, or are you hesitant when you get into a new situation, when you enter someone's office for the first time, a new store, a new friend's house? Are your gestures uncertain or definite? Do you shake hands firmly or limply? What is the overall impression your walk and movements make on others?

Knowing this will help you to understand how much power you project, but this is probably the most difficult area in which to achieve objectivity. You can sometimes solve this by seeing yourself through the eyes of a good and trusted friend—rarely through the eyes of a lover. Lovers are too emotionally involved to see you as you are. The same is true of your parents and your children, your brothers, sisters or close relatives.

In asking a friend to evaluate your body movement in terms of power, give him a scale of one to ten and ask him to place you somewhere along that line. When he's done this, try to pin him down to just what it is about you that he considers weakest. Your walk? Your posture? Your gestures? Then concentrate on that one element and try to improve it, to push it up the scale towards ten.

It won't be easy and you won't change at once. There must be enough time for feedback to take over, for whatever improvement you have decided on to become a normal part of your movements. But once you have started the change, any further changes will become increasingly easy.

"Of all our recent presidents," a politician told me, "I would consider Johnson the one who was most comfortable with power, who knew how to really use it to whip Congress into shape. His power plays in Washington gave him the ability to get almost any bill he wanted passed.

"I won't go into the lurid methods he used—there were so many factors involved. He knew men's weaknesses and strengths, and he used them unmercifully, but one thing about him that impressed me was the way he shook hands."

"What do you mean?" I asked.

"He wasn't content to just shake your hand. He'd shake with his right hand while his left grabbed your arm just above the elbow and gave it an additional squeeze."

"I've heard newspaper reporters call that pressing the flesh."

"Whatever they call it, it worked. The double touch gave you a feeling of sincerity. You suddenly believed, whether it was true or not, that this man liked you, liked you enough to touch you in two places. You felt that handshake, and you were in his power!"

There is indeed a power to touch, and in our society touch is a function of status. People who are rich, old and male have the social right to touch those who are poor, young and female. This was brought out by a study done at Harvard University some time ago.

A psychologist, Dr. Nancy H. Henley, went out to shopping malls, stores, subways—all the public places where people congregated, and she kept notes on who touched whom. She found that among strangers, there were many more cases of men touching women then of women touching other women, of men touching other men, or of women touching men. Men, she concluded, feel that they have the power to touch women.

She found out that older people touched younger people more often than the younger touched the older, and rich touched poor more often than poor touched rich. We are a touching society, but our touching follows a power-based formula. Those with the greatest amount of power seem to feel that they have the right to touch those with lesser power.

In the family set-up, the same status-power-touch system prevails. It is the parents who initiate touching, though it is the children who have the greater need for it. The parents also dictate how much touching there should be. The child who equates touching with cuddling and love may ask for the touching, but if the parent, for one reason or another, is unable to give it, the child may grow up with a sense of emotional deprivation.

"My husband complains that I never reach out to touch him, to initiate lovemaking," a young woman told me. "But he doesn't understand how hard it is for me to do it. I was never touched by my parents when I was a child, and if I tried to touch them first they moved away. That rejection had a terrible effect on me. Ever since I've been afraid to risk being the toucher. If I tried to touch my husband, it would give him too much power over me."

"What kind of power?"

"The power to reject me. I think I would want to

die if I ever touched him and he moved away!''

She saw power only in his acceptance of rejection, but she was the one who was playing the power game by withholding touch.

When I was a young man, I was a counselor at a boys' camp where many of the campers came from unhappy, broken homes. I vividly recall two incidents. One young child, whenever I was talking to someone and he was nearby, would come up and maneuver himself next to me in such a way that my hand brushed his head. Without thinking, I would ruffle his hair and give him a little caress when he did this. After awhile I became aware how much that touch meant to him, how much it put him in my power.

Another incident was the evening storytelling session. I'd sit on one of the children's beds after lights out and tell a story, and whose bed I sat on was a cause of bitter rivalry. It meant that the child could cuddle up to me and receive an extra session of touching. Again there was a power element. I could command all sorts of behavior by that prize. I could sit on the bed of the boy with the neatest bunk, the one who didn't fight all day, the one who wrote the longest letter home. Love and affection, interpreted as touch, gave me the power.

In an adult-child relationship, the power is almost always with the adult, and the decision to touch or not to touch is the adult's prerogative. I have seen teachers in school use this very calculatingly to gain power over the students. I knew one young man who taught a class of eight-year-olds in a private school. He would walk up and down the aisle as he lectured to them, and he would stop at the desks of his favorite pupils and either tousle their hair or grip their shoulder for a moment.

From the pleased, sometimes self-conscious and sometimes delighted smiles, I realized that this was his way of dispensing rewards for work well done. The power he used was reward power, and the students competed with each other for that tactile moment.

The same equation, touch-equals-love and affection-equals-power, can operate in the business world. I was recently given a tour of the art department of a large printing plant by one of the owners. From time to time he would stop at one desk or another to explain the work to me, and each time he would touch the shoulder or arm of the worker—using this power to bestow a reward. "I like you enough to touch you," was the clear, unspoken message, and I noticed the same pleased smiles on the men's faces that I had seen on the students' faces when the teacher rewarded them with a touch. The owner, incidentally, was older by a decade than any of the printers. I don't know if the same reward would have worked if a younger man tried it. Remember, age has status.

What it all adds up to—eye contact, spatial maneuvering, gesture, touch—is the fact that power can be expressed through body language. This isn't done in the manipulative way of convincing another person of your importance, but in terms of convincing yourself, through improved body language, that you can be more powerful than you are.

Dr. William C. Schutz, the author of *Joy*, has suggested that our psychological attributes affect our body function, and Dr. Ida Rolf has gone on to speculate that emotions harden the body into set patterns. She has even developed a "Rolfing" technique of deep massage for loosening up these hardened patterns.

Dr. Alexander Lowen, in his book *Physical Dynamics of Character Structure* takes all of this a step beyond and comes up with the concept that all neurotic problems are shown by the structure and function of the body. If you can change the way the body functions, you can change the man. Power, too, is reflected in our body stance, structure and function—in our body language. But power is amenable to change. Change your body language in the directions we have discussed in this chapter, and you will begin to strengthen your own inner sources of power.

Speaking of Power

Linda, one of the most powerful women I know, in terms of personality, sheer drive and ability, runs a very successful business in a small city on the West Coast. She knows what she wants and goes after it with a surprising amount of determination—which is surprising, because to listen to her you would never guess that she was as competent, knowledgeable and shrewd as she is.

Physically, Linda is an attractive woman, slim and well dressed, but when she begins to speak, she becomes a bewildered paradox. This sensible, no-nonsense woman has a little girl's voice, high pitched and shrill, a voice you associate with a flirt or a featherbrain.

145

"When I first heard her talk," a business associate told me, "I figured she was a piece of fluff. She was selling a small apartment house in Oakland, and I really wanted that property. I thought she'd be a pushover, but I came out of that deal paying a hell of a lot more than I ever intended to—and angry as hell."

"Why angry?" I asked.

"Because I felt cheated. Here was this woman with a silly little voice, and behind that voice was a will of iron—I just won't deal with her again."

"I know my voice is a problem," Linda told me almost a year ago. "But it has its advantages. It disarms the men I'm dealing with. It makes them think they can take advantage of me, and they let their guard down—enough for me to get what I'm after." She hesitated. "The trouble is, it has its disadvantages too, and that's why I'd like to do something about it, maybe change it."

"What are the disadvantages?" I asked.

She shrugged. "The men I deal with feel as if I've manipulated them, in a sense I guess I have. They judge me by my voice, not by my ability. Then, when I prove that I'm capable, they think I'm taking unfair advantage of them. But they're the ones that see me as a little girl. Is that dishonest?"

Reluctantly, I had to admit that in a sense she was. Her voice gave a false picture to the men she dealt with, and I thought she was wise to do something about it. I helped her find a good voice coach, and we explained the problem.

The coach, a former Hollywood actress, nodded. "There is no question that your voice is a major factor in how others see you," she said.

"Remember the Shaw play, *Pygmalion,* the one they turned into *My Fair Lady*? Well, in the play Professor Higgins takes a cockney flower girl and turns her into a lady by changing her voice and her way of speaking. It's true, the voice identifies us on a social plane—oh, less in America than in Europe—but still we are what we say, or we should be, and from what you tell me, you are not."

I met Linda a year later on one of my trips to the West Coast, and we had dinner together. The voice lessons had been successful, and she had managed to lower her pitch considerably. "I've also learned to resonate from the chest," she told me proudly in a low, well-modulated voice.

"Your voice has changed for the better, but has anything else changed?"

"Only my life!" She laughed. "It's amazing what's happened in my business in the past months. We're expanding like crazy. Customers return and recommend me to other people. But the best thing is the attitude of the men I deal with. They treat me as an equal now, as someone they can respect. Before, they would never take me seriously. They used to flirt and tease—" She hesitated. "It's really strange."

"What is?"

"Why how much difference lowering my voice has made, how much more powerful I seem in all business relations."

What Linda had learned is that there is a voice of authority, a voice of power. It speaks from the chest rather than from the nasal passages, and it is lower in pitch and fractionally slower than normal.

I spoke to a man in a midwestern television station who had just been made part of the news team, and he knew exactly what this "voice of power" meant. "I wanted this job," he told me, "and I knew I had the ability and the appearance. Oh, appearance is important in television work, of course, but voice quality if even more important, and do you know, it took me a month before I was able to get just the right voice quality?"

When I asked what that was, he frowned a bit. "A newscaster has to suggest authority, and that means lowering the pitch of your voice, resonating from the chest, controlling your speed and sometimes clipping your words slightly. That can add an edge of excitement to your speech."

Of the many factors that make up the human voice, pitch is one of the most significant, but a loud voice is also a power-grabber. You can shout someone else down if you're loud enough, but under certain circumstances, a soft voice can be even more powerful. The trick to achieving power with a soft voice is to have enough clout so that people will listen.

Resonance gives quality to a voice and depends on which space of the body we use as a sounding board. Resonate through your nose and your voice takes on a whine or a supercilious air, but change your resonance to your chest and your voice is rich, powerful, vibrant and masculine.

The speed at which we speak also affects the message behind our words. Rapid speech gives a sense of urgency, drama and eagerness. Too rapid, however, and the voice turns impatient, disorganized, even a bit wild. The slow talker can project thoughtfulness and commitment, but talking too slowly will signal reluctance and indifference—even backwardness.

The Family Dictator

But of course it is more than the sound of the voice that denotes power. It is also what the voice says. "When my father spoke," Elaine told me, "the family moved. There was no doubt about who had the power in the family, who ruled the roost! I remember so many times when my mother would be close to tears pleading with my brother and me to do something. 'Children, will you *please* pick up your toys.' or 'Won't you turn off the TV and go to bed? It's very late.' or 'Can't you clean up your rooms!' and we'd just sort of ignore her and keep on with what we were doing. Oh, I don't think it was deliberate on our part—we really loved her, but we never seemed to hear her until she finally exploded or began to cry. Then we were always ashamed of ourselves, and we'd scurry around trying to make up."

"But with my father there was never any question. 'Put away your toys!' or 'Turn off that set!' He didn't ask us to do things. He told us to do them, and in no uncertain terms—and we obeyed without question!"

Elaine's memories of her childhood seemed balanced between her mother's vague pleadings and her father's dominate orders. She left home in her early twenties and worked for three years before she met the man she married. "We wanted a family and Bob didn't see the point of my working, so I gave it up—a little reluctantly because I liked the work and I thought we could use the extra money. But Bob was very definite, and, of course, after our first child was born there seemed no time for anything but the home and family."

It wasn't until they had been married for seven years that Elaine became aware of just how unhappy she was in her marriage. "But by then there were two children and I couldn't see any possible way of changing. Besides, I loved Bob."

"But you were unhappy?"

"You know, it's something that was there all along, but it took me all those years to realize it. I had married Bob because in many ways he reminded me of my father. He had the same ability to command respect from people. Everyone looked up to him and admired him the way they used to look up to Dad. It was only recently that I realized the very thing I admired in Bob—his power—made me miserable."

Noticing my bewilderment, she smiled. "Let me put it this way. I never had any choice with Bob. Just the way it used to be with Dad. Bob never asked me what I wanted to do, he told me. It would be, 'We're going out to dinner with the head of marketing and his wife. Get a baby sitter,' or 'We'll drive up to the lake country for our vacation,' or 'We're going to stay home this weekend. We've been running around enough.' At first I used to think he was masterful, and then I realized he was simply dictatorial."

"What did you do?"

"Well, when I told him how I felt he was genuinely bewildered. I said, "We never do what I want,' and he said, 'Don't you want to do what we do?' How could I make him see it wasn't the same thing?"

"Did you?"

"I think so. Bob is a very decent person, and we love each other. It's just, well, he's a very powerful

150

person too, and I had to make him understand that he mustn't use that power with me—or with our children. Now don't get me wrong. I'm proud of the way he uses power. It's gotten us to where we are now, but it's something that must be used carefully. Thank heaven Bob is smart enough to understand that and try to change; otherwise, I don't think our marriage would survive.''

The change Elaine is asking of Bob is far more difficult than the change Linda made. She was able to turn her little girl's voice into a mature one, but Elaine is asking Bob to change more than his voice. It is his entire attitude to her and the children that she wants him to re-evaluate. Bob has developed a verbal approach that matches his inner assurance. He is direct and to the point and asks for what he wants.

Elaine, like her mother, qualifies every request she makes. "It was a good movie, wasn't it?" The *wasn't it* takes the positive edge off her statement. "I think that shirt looks good on you." The *I think* waters down her compliment. Most women, like Elaine, tend to use these qualifiers, and it is one of the cultural differences in men's and women's speech. Qualifiers send out messages of insecurity and uncertainty. The woman who rises to a positive of power quickly learns to discard them. Rather than asking Bob to be less dominant, Elaine would do well to learn how to use some power herself, to say quite simply, "It was a good movie," or "That shirt looks good on you," or, when Bob dictates his wishes about a vacation, to say, "I want to go to the beach this summer."

Another aspect of power in speech is the ability to make your presence felt. When Bob and Elaine go to a party, she watches the gathering for at least fifteen minutes before she finds a group she can join. Bob walks into the room and up to the first group he sees. He puts out his hand and says, "Hi. My name is Bob," and he's into things at once.

"I don't know how to get the nerve to do it," Elaine tells him. "I'd feel terrified that people would just turn away and ignore me."

Bob shrugs. "Let them. I'd just walk over to someone else, but it never happens. That's just your insecure fantasy. I want to know people and have them know me, and I make it happen. That's all."

The difference between them, of course, is a matter of basic security. Bob has it, Elaine hasn't, and their speech patterns reflect both conditions.

6

RISKING

Nothing Ventured, Nothing Gained

A group of us were sitting on the deck of my friend Merton's house, watching the sun set over the Pacific one evening. Merton, who had been tossing pennies into the bubbling hot tub claiming it acted as a wishing well, said, "I saw a job I could apply for the other day. Selling business machines. It said absolutely no experience needed. They have their own list of customers."

His wife, Connie, sipped her drink. "He's been like that ever since we sailed back from England on the *QEII*. He complained about the first-class service all the way."

I smiled. Merton was a compulsively successful Hollywood writer who had once confessed to me that he had more money than he knew what to do with. "So you're job hunting," I said.

"Well—I read the want ads. There was one for a retired couple to look after an estate out in the valley, but Connie says I'm not retired yet." He tossed another coin into the hot tub. "You know, I never had a job, a real job. I started writing and selling when I was a kid, and I was making a hundred a week in the middle of the Depression.

Whenever we got together, my Dad used to ask me when I was going to get a real job. He'd come up with some position he'd heard about that paid forty or fifty dollars a week, but as he pointed out, it was *real* work." He hesitated, then in a serious voice, added, "I guess what I want to find out is whether I have the power to work."

That interested me. I asked, "Why do you say *power*?"

"Perhaps because I've never worked at a job, as such. That takes a kind of power. It's a risk, isn't it?"

We were silent for a moment, then Larry, an executive with a large industrial corporation, cleared his throat. "I think the risk is in changing jobs. I did a few years ago. I used to be a hospital administrator, and while I was good at it, I felt limited. I thought I was going nowhere. But you know, I had no experience outside of hospital administration. My first job was doing their P.R. work and I worked my way up inside the hospital hierarchy. The trouble was, I wanted something else, a position with more responsibility, more power too, and I knew I couldn't get it in the hospital."

"What did you do?" Connie asked.

"I picked the biggest corporation in my area and I walked into the office of the president and I asked for a job as his assistant."

"Just like that?"

"Exactly. I knew I was taking a risk, but I also knew that if it paid off it would be worth it."

"What happened?"

"He talked to me for a while, then, with a rather cold look, said, "You know, this job requires a tremendous amount of experience in corporate management and a Ph.D. in economics.''

''Well, I think I was pretty cool myself when I answered, 'I've got neither,' and you know, an hour later I had the job!''

We were all silent for a moment, and then Merton said, ''I appreciate the drama of the situation, but why the hell did he hire you?''

''Self-confidence,'' Larry said. ''I told him I could do the job, and do it better than any other applicant, and I convinced him. I convinced him because I had convinced myself I could do it. It was a management job, and I was a damned good manager. My record at the hospital showed that. I was willing to take a chance at something else, a risk really, because we both agreed that if I didn't work out in one month I'd be out on my can. But I really felt the risk was worth it.'' He lit a cigarette and looked at Merton through the smoke. ''Do you honestly feel that the risk of trying to work at a job at your age, of testing yourself, is really worth it?''

Merton tossed another coin towards the hot tub. ''I don't know,'' he said thoughtfully. ''I've got to think that through.''

I never found out if Merton took that particular risk. If he has, he hasn't let anyone know, but I rather suspect that he hasn't. It was just a fantasy with him. There was no economic force driving him, nor was there the same thing that pushed Larry—the spirit of adventure, the need for wider opportunities, a chance at power. The jobs Merton was talking about were all close to the bottom of the economic ladder. If he ever took one, it would be only as a test of his ability to hold down a job, any nine-to-five job, and he was already at the top of the ladder in his own field. He had made it to the head of his profession, screenwriting.

But some weeks ago I read in *Variety* that Merton had indeed taken a risk, a long shot, motivated by the same spirit of adventure that moved Larry, the need for wider horizons. Instead of selling his latest screenplay, Merton had decided to produce and direct his film himself. The point of it all, according to the article, was that now Merton would have complete control over his story, the ability to produce it his way, as he saw it. He had the power, and along with it the responsibility of the production and the risk of failure.

All of us, no matter what level we operate on, must learn that risking is a very risky business. We cannot gain power in a business or in a personal relationship unless we are willing to chance something—and also, unless we are willing to be responsible for our risks. Before you take a risk, you must know what the consequences of that step are. Before Larry gave up his job as hospital administrator to become assistant to the president of a large corporation, he had to know just what would happen if he failed.

Not all risks succeed. Larry did well, but it's possible that he could have fallen into water over his head. In a sink-or-swim situation he could have sunk. He could have found himself with a job he couldn't manage, and, after a month, without either job. He knew it was a possibility, part of the risk, and when I asked him about it later, he admitted it.

"You just can't go around taking risks like I took in the job world. You have to be responsible for your actions, or you can end up getting your head chopped off. Look, I knew exactly what I was doing and what the odds were. First of all, trying to get in to see the president isn't easy. I could have been tossed out on my ass. If he had laughed at me it would have been a humiliating experience, a real bummer. Maybe I was lucky. The risk worked for me, but I knew I could handle the job. You see, if I had loused up I'd be out pounding the pavements, but I was willing to give it the old college try." He shrugged. "Besides, my wife was right behind me. She said, go ahead."

Once you know the risk you are taking, once you decide to take responsibility for that risk and all its consequences to your family as well as yourself, then—and only then—do you have the right to take that risk. I am sure my friend Merton knew the risk he was taking when he started his own picture company, and I am also sure he balanced the power he wanted against the chance of failure. I am also sure he came up with that ultimate answer to any question about risk: *Nothing ventured, nothing gained*!

Risking Intimacy

We have considered risking on a business level in order to become more powerful in the job market, or to gain power over your own creative product as in Merton's case. These are valid risks, but just as much risking goes on in our lives on a personal level.

Perry is a bachelor in his mid-thirties and he's been seeing a therapist for the past few months.

Perry is relatively successful at his work, though he's changed jobs twice in the last two years. In each case it was a change that worked out. "I'm not afraid of taking a gamble at work," he told his therapist. "What the hell, what have I got to lose? I'm young and healthy and I know my field. But the thing that gets me is that I can't seem to take a chance with a woman. I'm afraid to risk intimacy. I'll meet someone, and she'll seem perfect in every way, and then, after a month or so, I'll blow the whole deal."

"In what way?"

"Oh, I don't know. I'll say the wrong thing, or do the wrong thing, hurt her in some way, and then, even when I've realized what I've done, I don't seem able to say, 'I'm sorry.' To put things right."

"It sounds to me," his therapist said, "as if you're trying to destroy the relationship before it gets too deep."

Perry couldn't accept that at first, but a few sessions later he came back to it. "What I think I'm afraid of," he admitted, "is opening myself up, trusting another person."

"But why?"

Quietly, Perry answered, "If I trust someone, let her see how much I care, and then she decides to walk out of me, I'll be the one with egg on my face."

"And is that so bad?" the therapist asked. When Perry started to protest, he said, "There used to be a song when I was a kid, how did it go? It is better to have loved and lost than never to have loved at all. Remember that, Perry."

It was pretty corny, Perry thought, but it came back to him a week later. He had met a young woman he liked at the health club, and they had gone out together a few times and everything seemed to be going well. Then the inevitable happened. Going home one night, Petty said the wrong thing, and the woman froze up. At her door he asked, "Do you want me to come in?" and she shook her head. "Don't bother!"

It seemed the usual end to an affair, but this time Perry decided he was going to risk a rejection. He put his hand on her arm and said, "Hey, I didn't mean what I said. I act like a damned fool sometimes. Forgive me? Please . . ."

The girl hesitated for a moment, and Perry felt a terrible emptiness inside him. This was the hardest thing he had ever done, and sweat stood out on his forehead. Then she smiled and said, "Oh, let's forget it. Come in and have a drink."

"And if she had said, 'Get lost,' " his therapist asked at their next session, "what would have been so terrible about that? You took a risk. It paid off, fine. But if it hadn't, would you have been any worse off than if you never apologized?"

In any kind of risking, the fear of rejection is a powerful obstacle. Perry believed that apologizing for what he had said left him vulnerable. He could be easily hurt. Why risk it? He had always been afraid to risk intimacy for fear of being hurt, and as a result he had suffered the greater hurt of loneliness. "Nothing comes easy," his therapist told him. "If you want someone to love you, you have to take a chance. The deeper the love you're after, the greater the chance."

He might have also said, *the deeper the love, the more you have to lose*. I knew a very popular doctor in his eighties who was still unmarried. I interviewed him once about some work he was doing, and I asked him why he had never married.

"Because I couldn't ever bear the idea of loving someone and then losing them," he told me very seriously. "Suppose I committed myself to a woman and married her. Eventually I might run the risk of losing her through death or desertion. I couldn't bear that."

I was amazed that so intelligent and talented a man had gone through life alone and lonely rather than risk commitment and love. In some ways it was like the person who commits suicide because he can't bear the thought of dying, or the artist who never tries to create because he might not reach a certain standard of excellence, or the writer afraid to write a book because the critics might destroy it. Apply that same fear of risking to any part of life and it must eventually lead to sterility and a dead end.

The Fear of Risking

Sometimes we risk because we know it's the only way to get what we want, and sometimes we risk because we have no other choice. But there are times when a risk doesn't seem worth taking. Harold, a widower in his fifties, was afraid that if he told his daughter Ellen what he really felt, he'd risk losing her.

Ellen was twenty-one, a very pretty girl and a very talented musician. She was going through college on a scholarship, and she worked evenings playing the piano at a small dinner club. It paid her tuition and expenses, but it wasn't enough to pay for an apartment. She had been happy enough living at home until she met Jim, another music student.

"Jim and I want to move in together," she told her father. "Share an apartment."

"You mean, live together?" Harold asked, fighting back his shock. "You don't mean getting married?" he added hopefully.

"Oh, Daddy!" Ellen said it with just that tone of despair calculated to make any parent cringe. "We're both grown up. We're old enough to know what we want to do. I'm asking you to help me out, financially. You've always told me to come to you with any problem, and this is a real problem. Jim and I can't make it on our own, even pooling our money."

"That was the point," Harold admitted, "at which my immediate impulse was to snap back. *If you're old enough to know what you want to do, you're old enough to find some way of doing it on your own.* I thought that was pretty good. Or I could have tried, *If you can't make it on your own, maybe you shouldn't make it at all.* I must confess I was shocked. My wife and I grew up in a different world with different standards. I knew that, but are those standards wrong? Or are the ones Ellen and Jim go by?

"Still, I knew that if I acted on impulse, I stood a good chance of losing Ellen, especially if she really loved this guy she wanted to move in with. Emotion told me to disapprove, but logic said, if Ellen loves him and wants to live with him, she will, somehow or other, no matter what I told her. Now if I help her, I still function as her father. I still have some influence over her.

"I knew she needed my approval, my love, and

that need gave me a kind of power. You've got to remember, the power to give love and approval is tremendous, just as tremendous as the power to withhold it!''

Harold's decision turned out to be right for him. He wanted to keep Ellen's love, and he knew she needed his. He helped her out with a monthly allowance and discovered, to his surprise, that he liked Jim, and it was easy to accept him. "The only problem I faced," he confessed, "was how to introduce him to my friends. *My daughter's lover*? Too old-fashioned. *Her roommate?* Silly, really. *Her friend*? That didn't even begin to describe the relationship. I finally settled for just plain Jim, and I introduced him like that. Let everyone draw his own conclusions.''

Harold's risk was hard enough, but in a way Ellen's was even harder. "I took a big chance when I confronted Dad with my decision," she pointed out. "He's a pretty old-fashioned guy in many ways—at least his values are. I knew that there was always the possibility that he wouldn't be able to accept my life style. What really scared me was that I might have to choose between Dad and Jim. I really love Dad. Boy, parents have a lot of power over you. Even after you've grown up you still need to know they care about you.''

In a sense, Harold's refusal to risk alienating Ellen allowed him to retain some of his influence over her, but at the same time he was able to abdicate some of his parental power. One of the hardest things a parent faces is giving up parental power. It means that we must accept the fact that our children have become adults.

As adults, they might still be influenced, but it

would be a wrong use of power to try to run their lives, to dictate their life styles or choices of partners. Once Harold gave up that power, Ellen was able to assume the responsibility for her own life. It was an exchange of power, but not a complete one, for Ellen still needed her father's love and approval just as he needed hers.

Your Inner Risk Factor

For some of us, risk-taking is a simple adding up of all the advantages and disadvantages, and then making a choice between them. But many of us cannot make that choice. We need the inner power to take the risk. How do you discover whether you are strong enough to take risks? How do you determine your own *inner risk factor*?

You can do it through an evaluation of your own life and the number of times you gambled on important issues. Another help in determining it is a simple test. I have prepared ten questions, each with three possible answers. The only thing required is that you answer each question with absolute honesty.

To answer honestly, you must put aside all concerns about right or wrong, all questions of morality. You may feel that one is the right answer, but the point is, what would *you* do, not what is *right* to do. No one is judging your answers except yourself.

1) You attend a convention in Nevada and you must pass a bank of slot machines each day on your way to the meeting hall.

> (A) You put all your quarters in each time you
>   go past.
> (B) You set aside an alloted amount to play
>   with and stick to that amount.
> (C) You ignore the machines. You're here for
>   the convention.

2)   You're a man and you like the way a bright red
tie looks with your suit, or if you are a woman, you
have just bought a rather daring blouse that should
be unbuttoned to the cleavage.

> (A) You decide to wear it to work.
> (B) You won't wear it to work, but you will
>   wear it socially.
> (C) You return it the next day and wonder
>   what silly impulse made you buy it in the
>   first place.

3)   Have you ever made sexual overtures to a partner?

> (A) Directly?
> (B) Indirectly?
> (C) Not at all!

4)   You're working at a job and your supervisor is
obnoxious.

> (A) You tell him off.
> (B) You treat him cooly.
> (C) You pretend there's nothing wrong.

5)   You meet a stranger on a plane and she/he is
attractive, but you know nothing about him/her.
She/he suggests that you meet for dinner that
night.

> (A) Sure. It might be fun.

(B) You sugggest a foursome with a couple
    you know.
(C) Absolutely not.

6)   You go to the race track with a friend and he
points out that "Flash Freeze" in the fourth race is
a sure thing at twenty-to-one.
    (A) You put down twenty dollars.
    (B) You bet a moderate five.
    (C) You realize that betting is for suckers.

7)   The company you work for is relocating to a
new area you know nothing about. You're good in
your field, and they offer you better pay to
relocate.
    (A) You take it. It could be a good place to
        live and the salary is worth it.
    (B) You spend ever minute down to the wire
        trying to guess which is right, go or stay,
        and eventually you go because who knows
        if another job is available here?
    (C) You decide not to go because you're too
        attached to the house and town you live in.
        You start job hunting.

8)   You're with a group of friends discussing
politics, and they mention a candidate whose name
is totally unfamiliar.
    (A) You ask who he is.
    (B) You join in carefully hoping your ignor-
        ance won't be detected.
    (C) You keep your mouth shut till the subject
        changes.

9)   You're looking for a vacation spot and some-

one tells you of a fabulous place he's gone to and urged you, if you want to go, to make a reservation at once. They're almost full up.

(A) You take his advice and make the reservation.

(B) You ask for more details and the names of other people who liked it before you decide.

(C) You settle for a place you know.

10) Your boss gives you an order you know is wrong.

(A) You question the order and tell him why.

(B) You do as he tells you, but feel uneasy all day. What if he finds out and blames you?

(C) You obey the order, but look for some way of covering up repercussions.

Scoring

You should give yourself ten points for every (A) answer, eight for all the (B)'s and six for the (C)'s. If you get a score of 80 to 100, you are considered quite a gambler. Between 70 and 80 indicates someone who will take a sensible amount of risks, and a score of 60 to 70 indicates that you are in some trouble in terms of risk-taking. Since you cannot get power without taking risks, the obvious question now is do you want power? If you do, you must learn to risk.

Learning to Risk

So you're determined that you want to operate from a position of power, that you want more control over your life. You want to change your job or move out on your own and be more independent of your husband or your wife. You want to take that chance to go into business or declare yourself a political candidate or try that difficult grant or change professions. It's all well and good to make the decision to do any one of these things—it's quite another matter to take the risk. You've tested yourself and you score a slim 60. You're obviously a person who doesn't gamble, who's afraid to take a chance and has always played it safe.

There are many reasons to fear risking, and the most common one is the fear of failure or the humiliation of being rebuffed. People who honestly score 100 on the risking test have none of these fears. Perhaps they are unrealistic. A successful businessman, chairman of the board of a large drug firm, came up with a score of 80. He told me, "I've usually gone for the long shots. If I fail, so what? Am I any worse off than before? Failure is a part of the game. If you're afraid to fail, then you're afraid to try, and you're lost. You've got to understand that most failures don't mean anything. You pick yourself up, dust yourself off and start over. Listen, for every success I've had I've also had a half dozen flops, but in the long run I've gotten ahead."

"All well and good," the timid starter says. "He can talk. He scored eighty. But I can never summon up enough courage to take the kind of chance that might change my life. What can I do?"

What we all can do if we are afraid of risking, is start small. Most people who can take risks learn the art as children. If they succeed in their first risks, they go on to bigger and better ones. If they don't succeed, if they're knocked down again and again, they grow fearful of trying and they end up as timid starters.

Now the timid starter has to make up for all those early failures. He can do it best by starting with an easy risk. The meaningless risk. You'll do this one on the telephone to avoid any face-to-face confrontation and the possibility of being overawed by someone else's manipulative body language. As we suggested earlier in the book, try bucking the bureaucracy. Call the phone company about a mischarged call, or the utility company, or even a credit card outfit. Let yourself get angry, and if you wish, hang up on them. That's a tickle of power!

What have you accomplished? Well, for one thing you've gotten your feelings out, expressed hostility or anger, and *survived*. That's something.

Now you're prepared to risk a face-to-face confrontation. Try it first with a stranger in a situation that isn't important. Get into an argument with a shopkeeper or with a waiter in a restaurant. Send back a dish that isn't done properly. This takes a surprising amount of courage. Argue with a supermarket clerk about the price of an item, a price that's been raised while it's on the shelf. Or get into a cab and tell the driver the exact route you want him to take to get you where you're going—your way, not his! You may win out in some of these arguments, though it's a rare person who can win over a cab driver or a waiter. But the whole point of these confrontations is to experience failure as well as success, to learn that losing is not the end of the world.

Once you're really comfortable with these introductory warm-up exercises in asserting your own will, you're ready to move on to some serious risking. In effect you've tested your wings and found that you can fly—or flop. While victory may have been less satisfying than you thought it would be, failure may not be as devastating as you expected. Survival is the key, and if you've survived the warm-up, then you're ready for some Class C risks.

(1) Tell somebody off, whether it's a co-worker, your mate, your neighbor, your brother, sister, parent, or even your child. It shouldn't be someone with power over you, but an equal.

(2) Make your husband or wife or lover do something *you* want, something they're not eager to do. Perhaps to buy something or go somewhere, to see a certain movie or watch a television program. The point is, it must be something *you* want.

(3) If you work, ask your boss or supervisor for the day off for personal matters. Refuse to give a reason. Say you simply want the time off.

(4) If you are unmarried, accept a blind date.

In all of these, failure is as important as success because part of the risking program is to understand that the world doesn't end, the sky doesn't fall in, you can still show your face when someone says no. On the other hand, you must learn to experience that little surge of power without guilt when it all works out.

If you have survived the Class C risks, you're ready to try your luck with the Class B series. Again, don't move from one series to the next until you're comfortable.

(1) If you are single, risk going to a single's bar and talking to at least five strangers. If one appeals to you, suggest a date. If singe's bars turn you off, try picking someone up at a social gathering, a museum or a movie.

(2) Ask your boss for a raise. Explain that you realize this will mean more responsibility and you're prepared for it.

(3) Tell your husband that you've decided that you'll take the responsibility for paying all the bills. You'll handle the checking account and the budget. No reasons. You've decided you want the responsibility.

(4) If you are a woman, initiate lovemaking with a physical overture.

(5) If you're a man, tell your lover just what you like in sexual lovemaking.

If you've come past Class B risking intact, and you've been able to think up five other risks on the same level and have tried them all, then you're ready for Class A. These are higher risks and should not be taken lightly. You must be sure you want them and are ready for their dangers as well as their rewards. Of course, no one takes all of them, but at least one (or a very similar risk) is necessary to demonstrate the two fundamental rules of power. You cannot get power without a risk, and you can survive the failure of any risk.

(1) Change your job if you don't like what you're doing. This risk is linked to age. In the twenties it is almost a Class B risk. In the thirties it is more serious, but in the forties it is a full-fledged Class A. There are people who have changed jobs successfully in their fifties and sixties, but it is much harder, and far more is at risk then.

(2) Invest money. For some people this is so normal a procedure that they do not seriously consider it a risk. But they, of course, are used to taking risks. For anyone scoring only 60 on the risk factor test this is a definite Class A risk. Do it wisely, and be fully aware of the consequences.

(3) Buy a home or an apartment. Many people feel this risk is so great that they defer it all their lives. If you have sound reasons for not buying your home, or if you are a comfortable renter, try moving, changing neighborhoods. But again, there must be some advantage involved. You should not risk just for the sake of risking, but because in some way it will increase your power base.

(4) If you are a woman and have never worked, go out to get a job—with or without your husband's approval. The latter, of course, is a greater risk, and you get correspondingly more power from it if it works out!

(5) Give up your job and go into business for yourself. On a business level, this is one of the greatest risks of all and one you should never take without knowing all the consequences, all the possible dangers as well as advantages. Because the risk is so great, the power you achieve, if all goes well, is also on the highest level.

(6) Just as starting your business is the greatest risk on a business level, getting married is the

greatest risk on a personal level. Many people, however, would argue that staying single is a greater risk.

(7) If you are not, by sexual preference, heterosexual, come out of the closet and tell your parents or friends—or take another risk and tell the world.

7

COPING WITH POWER

A Little Stress Never Hurts

"My biggest problem," Kirk said, "is that I don't know how to cope with power."

Bill blew the foam off his beer and sighed. "You think that's a problem? Hell, I don't know how to get power, much less cope with it."

The three of us were in the dimly-lit bar celebrating Kirk's new promotion to head of his department, but somewhere during the evening the celebration had gone sour.

Bill went on in a gloomy voice. "The way I figure it, I must have been on the end of the line when they were passing out aggressive genes. No kidding, when I act like someone important I can never bring it off. I've tried all the one-upmanship games, and I'm always the one who gets put down. You wouldn't believe it, but I've even tried to imitate the way you dress, Kirk, and the result is a big fat zero! My father used to tell me, 'Bill, my boy, you just aren't a go-getter.' Now I have to admit that old man had my number."

"Maybe you're better off." Kirk was thoughtful. "You're looking at a real go-getter. Me. Here I am with my third promotion in two years, making a lot of dough, and you know what? I'm really running scared."

I got into the coversation then. "Why should you be scared?"

"Do you know what it means to be in a position where you have to make decisions every day that could mean thousands of dollars one way or the other? I've become one of the the most powerful guys in my firm, and I tell you I wake up at night in a sweat, wondering if I've goofed and cost the company a bundle. Even when I know I'm right, I feel under terrible pressure."

I shook my head and turned to Bill. "Do you feel that kind of pressure too? When he frowned, I added. "I mean on your job, like the stress Kirk is talking about?"

Bill grinned ruefully. "Not really. My job is pretty simple, and by now I've got it all under control. It's a piece of cake."

"Lucky guys!" Kirk said, sipping his beer. "I wish I had my job under control."

I thought about Bill and Kirk very seriously after that meeting. It seemed to me that they were on opposite ends of a stress scale. Kirk, a reasonably aggressive young man, had so much stress in his job that he could barely handle ut. Bill, on the other hand, led a relatively stressless life and seemed to have very little aggression. Kirk had always been able to cope with life. He had certainly made his way up the corporate ladder in a hurry, but once up it he didn't seem able to handle the problems that went with his job.

Bill had very little coping ability, not even enough to get started up the ladder, but he could manage his job. There is a connection between coping and power. They are both related to stress.

We usually think of stress as destructive. Medical authorities tell us that modern man is under too much stress. Unchecked, it leads to high blood pressure, heart attacks and emotional breakdowns. All this is true and too much stress is crippling my friend Kirk's life. He may indeed find himself in physical or emotional trouble while he's still a young man.

On the other side of the scale, Bill, exposed to little stress if any, seems caught in the backwater of a dull job and a low salary. A little more stress might present Bill with enough impetus to sharpen his coping skills and start him up the climb to power.

In small doses, stress triggers our coping ability, and coping alleviates stress. This low dose of stress powers the human condition and drives us to develop the skills we need to solve problems. When the amount of stress is reasonable, we move ahead. However, when the stress becomes too great, as it did with Kirk, we're in trouble. Sometimes we find that we cannot function at all.

While stress acts to help us develop our coping skills, we all react to stress differently. The pressure of inflation may cause one man to budget his money, another to look for a higher-paying job, a third to join a union to fight for higher wages and a fourth to blow his brains out because he cannot bear the pressure.

All four have coped with the situation, one in a disastrous way, the others by applying different coping skills to the problem. It is these skills that make all the difference between survival and destruction. In this chapter we'll consider a few of those skills and how we use them.

Aggression is one of the more basic skills in coping. Too often we think of aggression in a negative sense as a drive that leads to hostility, crime, violence and ultimately war. But this is aggression gone wild. We must also remember that aggression is behind most of the positive acts of life. When a family moves to a different neighborhood, the children who go out and make new friends are acting aggressively. The man or woman who goes after a good job is aggressive, and so is the successful salesman, politician, inventor, athlete, businessman, writer, artist—in fact, no progress or advancement could be made without aggression.

Exercising Your Assertion Muscles

"But what do you do," Sally, a young housewife, asked me, "if you have no aggression in you at all!"

"Oh, come on—everyone has some aggression . . ." I began.

"You think so, huh? You know, I decided to be more aggressive around the house. I was tired of my teen-age daughter borrowing my clothes without asking, my son bawling me out because I hadn't put enough mayo on his lunch sandwiches, my husband telling me I hadn't set the table with the dishes he likes—I was sick and tired of it, and I walked into the living room last night where everybody was watching "Charlie's Angels" and in my loudest voice I announced, 'I am my own woman! I will do what I like when I like it!'"

"What happened?"

"I had to repeat it three times before anyone

176

heard me and then my son said, 'Mom, I wish you'd stop mumbling,' and my husband said, 'Wait till the commercial, dear.' That did it. I marched back into the kitchen and smashed a dish, but big deal. I was acting aggressive to an inanimate object!"

I asked Dr. Fred Klein, a New York psychiatrist who is Director of the *Institute of Sexual Behavior* how someone like Sally could have increased her aggression.

"First of all," he said, "you don't start with a personal declaration of independence, and anyway, there is a real semantic problem with the word aggression. It's been linked to unpleasant things, to hostility and anger so much that people have trouble thinking of it in a positive way."

"How can you change what it's been linked to?"

"You can't, so I use a different word that means the same thing. I use assertion. That's a popular word nowadays. Assertion is in. Now from what you've told me, I believe your friend Sally's lack of assertiveness is a result of her poor self-image. She doesn't think a hell of a lot of herself. That's why she lets her family push her around. A poor self-image keeps you from coping with life. It's as simple as that."

Increasing the respect we feel for ourselves, Dr. Klein explained, can sharpen our coping skills. Good coping skills allow us to handle life more easily, to gain power when we want it and function to our fullest potential. That was really the answer to Sally's problem. She needed to respect herself, to see herself as an important person before she could begin to cope with her family again in an assertive way.

Encouraged by Dr. Klein's analysis of Sally's problem, I asked him about my two friends, Kirk and Bill. He nodded as I described our unhappy celebration.

"Your friend Bill, like Sally, has a poor self-image, and because of it he's not able to be assertive. That's what keeps him in the same rut year after year. Kirk, on the other hand, seems to have a healthy self-image and an ample amount of assertiveness."

"Then why is he having so much trouble now?"

Dr. Klein shrugged. "Not knowing him, I can guess that he lacks a number of coping skills. He does have one skill, assertiveness, and that's a good indication that he can learn the others. Your friend Bill, however, must learn to be assertive, and to do that he must strengthen his self-image."

"Can anyone do that?" I asked.

"Oh, yes. I teach my patients how to do it. I show them how to exercise their 'assertion muscles.' If I have a patient who's unassertive, I make him do what assertive people do as a matter of course."

"Could you describe some of those exercises?"

"Well, they vary according to the patient's problem. I've been treating one young man who has difficulty meeting women. He's not assertive enough, and he feels that he has no power over his own life. I give him some homework. 'At the next party you go to, walk up to at least two women you don't know and start talking to them.' It doesn't matter if they snub him. The idea is just for him to manage to talk to them. When he's done that I move him ahead. 'Go to a cafeteria and sit down at a table with a strange woman. Start talking to her.'

"If, on the other hand, someone has trouble

asking for things, I have her go to a coffee shop, sit at the counter and ask for a drink of water without buying anything."

"Hey, that's pretty rough!"

"For some people, yes. Others do it as a matter of course. But people who can't ask for things, who just aren't assertive enough, need that rough experience. I have other patients who have to learn to say no. If they're married and always give in to their partners, I tell them, 'Today, say no to at least one request.' I had a patient, a woman, who couldn't say no to her parents. They dropped in at awkward times, and she was at her wit's end. No matter how she tried, she couldn't bring herself to turn them away. Finally, one night when she felt she just had to be alone with her husband, she bought two tickets to a show, and when they turned up sent them off to the theatre. When I next saw her she told me she thought it was a cop-out, but I couldn't help noticing that she was exhilarated. In a sense she had denied them time with her and she had still survived. That was a positive step for her."

"Isn't that a lot like risking?" I asked, and I told him of the exercises I had developed for risking. "In a way they are smiliar," he agreed. "They're all designed for behavior modification. But these exercises are meant specifically for assertion. I also use *as if* situations. I have one patient who's afraid of his landlord. I'll make him ask for heat and act *as if* he's not scared, *as if* he were assertive."

"How do you do that?"

"There are four basic steps to acting assertively, to having another person perceive you as assertive.

(1) Look the other person in the eye. (2) Use a loud voice. (3) Hold yourself straight, and (4) Talk in full sentences. Do that to anyone, and you come across as an assertive person. You'll even *feel* assertive yourself and turn into a slightly more assertive person.

"There is one thing to remember," Dr. Klein told me after our talk. "People vary in their ability to absorb help, whether it's from therapists like me or from books written by you. I call it running with the ball. Some people pick up the merest hint of advice and carry it out to its logical end. They're born winners. They pick up the ball and go for a touchdown. Others must be told again and again before they can go the length of the field. If a reader of your book doesn't absorb the message the first time, he must be told it over and over and over."

"That makes for dull reading," I protested.

"The alternative is for him to read the same message again and again until he can finally pick up the ball and run with it," he laughed. "It depends on how bad his problem his."

The Flexible Woman

Assertiveness is an important coping tool, but it doesn't do much good unless it is combined with other coping skills. Maureen, a young executive from a midwestern city, combined her own assertiveness with a healthy amount of *flexibility*, another excellent coping skill. At a party given her in honor of a new promotion, she was approached by one of the other executives, Joe.

"You're not only one smart gal," Joe said, lifting his glass, "but a pretty lucky one, too. How about a little drink to that luck. Maybe some'll rub off on me—to a drink and a rub."

Maureen grinned. "I'll drink, but no rubbing. Anyway, it wasn't luck, Joe. It was just hard work, clean living—and being in the right place at the right time."

"Now that's what I mean by luck. Here you are, just about the only dame in this area with an MBA when the firm decides they want a woman executive. You gotta admit, that's luck."

Maureen looked at him quizzically, then shrugged. "I'll drink to my new job, Joe, but I won't drink to luck. You don't know the whole story!"

The "whole story" was what had made Maureen decide to go after a masters in business administration. She had graduated college as an English major and had gone on to graduate school to get her masters in seventeenth-century English poetry. It was after a year of graduate school that Maureen realized that there were practically no positions available in her field. As she told it, "Teaching had just about dried up, and it was then that I decided to drop out and change the whole direction of my life.

"My father said I was crazy to waste all that time I had put in. He said I was changing horses in midstream, and so I was, but when one set of horses becomes crippled you'd be crazy not to change. I got a job with a brokerage house for a year and I looked over the field. I saw how few women there were in business administration. So I made my decision. That year in business helped me get into a good MBA program, and I had saved enough from

181

the job to put myself through school. None of it was luck, and I could brain Joe for saying that!"

Maureen had managed to control her own life. She had been flexible enough to change once she became aware that she was headed in the wrong direction. It is this ability to control chance, to be aware of alternate solutions and to discard the bad ones while accepting the right ones that is a particularly effective coping tool.

Many of us link flexibility with vacillation. When I discussed flexibility with Kirk, my friend who had so much trouble coping with his high-pressured job, he said, "You make it sound like a positive attribute, but I think of it as a sign that a guy can't make up his mind. It's a weak trait, not a powerful one. Look! What it boils down to is that if a man can't get what he wants, he should settle for second best."

"Yes, you could label it a weakness, but turn it around and you can call it a strength."

"How?" Kirk asked challengingly.

"A flexible man doesn't limit himself. If he can't get what he's after, rather than butt his head against a wall, he takes what he can get."

It wasn't easy to convince Kirk, because this was one of the problems he was up against in his job. Time and again he was unable to do what he set out to. It took a series of talks to convince him that he had to re-evaluate his goals and question himself about their importance.

"You must ask yourself," I told him, "before you set any goal, how realistic is my attempt to reach it? No man in power should box himself in with unrealistic goals. But flexibility is more than this. You must search for alternative solutions.

182

"When you face a problem at work," I explained, "your first step must be to rest the reality of a solution. Can it be solved? If it cannot, then you must refuse to take it on. Your second step should be motivation, and this is where power enters the picture. If your motivation is powerful enough, you can solve any solveable problem. The final step is simply to list every possible approach to the problem, every possible solution, then choose the simplest."

I met Kirk a week after our last talk, and I was delighted to find that his troubled look was gone and his old assurance was back. "What happened?" I asked.

"Your advice finally sank in," he told me. "I'd been having so many problems on the job that I was about ready to give up. When I left you last week I went home and made a careful list of all the problems, then I crossed out all those that couldn't be solved. I wrote a memo on each explaining why nothing could be done about them, adding that it would only waste time, money and manpower to try. Then I took the solveable problems and decided that if power was what I needed, I damn well had it, anyway. Trying to do the impossible had been crippling me. I followed your suggestion, listed all my solutions, and in every case there was one easier than the others. I've solved two problems already, and I'm on my way to a solution of the third!"

"And the ones you wrote memos on?"

"That's the beautiful part. My boss agreed with me, and yesterday he called me in to tell me it was damned smart of me not to waste the company's time and money on blind alleys."

"So you're really on top of things."

"Let's just say I'm flexible about them!"

The Three Sides of Reason

Flexibility is a fine coping tool not only in business, but also in your personal life. To use flexibility properly, you must be able to judge all the different approaches to a problem, to evaluate them and select the best one. However, to do this properly you must use another coping tool, reason.

Reason is a three-sided tool, and one of its sides is *ambiguity*. Arthur was a man who was so assertive—though in his case, aggressive was a better word—that he had lost all sense of ambiguity. He ruled his family with an iron hand and a rigid code of morality, a sense of right and wrong that was so severe that he saw things only in black or white; for him, there were no grey areas.

For Arthur there were ony two ways of judging life—good or bad. When his oldest girl married a man without a job, Arthur was furious. "She's ruined her life. I told her not to marry him, and she deliberately disobeyed me. We're through!"

His wife tried to talk him out of it. Their daughter had a job, she pointed out, and eventually her husband would find work. They loved each other, and anyway, all of that was their own business.

Arthur brushed the arguments aside and refused to be anything more than coldly polite to his new son-in-law. Hurt by the way he treated her husband, his daughter cut herself off from the father. She continued to see her mother for lunch, but she never came back to the house.

Arthur wasn't much better with his son. When the boy wanted to drop out of college, Arthur saw it as the mark of a quitter. He laid down an ultimatum, "Leave school and you leave my house." His son left both, and two children were lost to him.

Arthur was a man with the potential for power, a strong, assertive man—but also a man who couldn't cope with power. His inability to see all the aspects of a problem, the fact that his daughter and her husband might have been right for each other, or that his son might find something besides college that was better for him, his refusal to see these other possibilities, diffused his power. In the end he was a man with no strength in his own family. His wife, who remained flexible and reasonable and accepted other viewpoints, was able to stay in touch with her children.

Most of us are not like Arthur. We understand that life exists in shades of grey, but still we are faced with newspapers, television and motion pictures that barrage us with a black and white world, a world of good guys or bad guys, of perpetrators and victims, rich and poor, those in the law and those outside the law.

It is only when we can see all the subtle shadings in between, all the different viewpoints possible and all the different alternatives, that we can be tolerant of others, understand them and use our power to work with or against them.

Stepping Back to Look Closer

A sense of ambiguity helps us to cope with life, but combine it with objectivity, the ability to step away from yourself and take a good hard look at what you're doing, and your coping ability becomes much stronger. "I am really in control of my life," my friend Jane told me confidently, "and you can put that control down to my objectivity."

Jane is an intelligent young woman who has a good secretarial job and a live-in roommate. "At least that's what I call John, my roommate. We have a good thing going. When I first suggested we live together, John was shocked. He has a lot of trouble with what you call ambiguity, seeing all sides of a problem. With him it was marriage or dating, either-or. I was tired of dating and not yet ready for marriage, and I wanted us to live together. It made sense, but I had a rough time getting him to see that. Well, I finally convinced him that there were alternatives to marriage, and being roommates wasn't a bad one—or at least I thought so at first."

"What made you change your mind?" I asked.

"A few things. One, I thought I was pregnant. It was a false alarm, but it suddenly occurred to me that if I was, if I had the baby, the legal tangle of parenthood would probably be a real mess. Then we had a chance to buy our apartment. It was a good deal, but again the legal hassle of two people owning property overwhelmed us. What if we split up?"

"It was at that point that I figuratively stepped back and took a rational look at our situation. From a distance, it didn't look half as good as it

186

had from up close. I began to wonder, considering all the alternatives, if I had been right to discard marriage. I finally decided that I had been a bit hasty, and I did it."

"Did what?"

"Got a long weekend, got married and went off on a short honeymoon."

"You said you were in control of your own life. Doesn't marriage weaken that control?"

"Not a bit. It strengthens it. By being in control I mean that I have the ability to rethink something I do, or decide if it isn't right for me. That's what I think of as control and power over yourself. It's not so much freedom—" She frowned for a moment. "It's more the recognition of necessity, of what you really need. It's kind of *second-chancing* it."

The right to a second chance, the power to change things that aren't quite good enough, is part of the benefit of objectivity—and a prerequisite of power.

Ambiguity and *objectivity* are only the first two steps in a three-part program that uses reason as a coping tool. To be used more efficiently, all three steps should be taken. Together they can not only give you power over your own life, as they did Jane, but also they can teach you how to use power properly.

The first step is ambiguity, to see all the possible ramifications of a problem. The second step is objectivity, the ability to step back and divorce yourself from the solution even as you realize how each solution will affect you.

The third step is discrimination, understanding which solution is better than any other. If you have any doubt, list them all and give each one a value. There will always be one that is best in terms of your own needs, or it may be best in terms of other's needs. Some choices will be best in terms of power. Which of the solutions you choose can only come from your inner direction, from your needs and desires and from the situation.

The Sensitive Salesman

In an attempt to find out what makes a powerful salesman, I talked to Murray, the head of sales for a large East Coast insurance company. "What is the chief quality that your high-pressure salesmen cultivate?" I asked him.

Murray leaned back and shook his head. "You're assuming a lot. First of all, why do you characterize a good salesman as high-pressured?"

I shrugged. "I just assumed—" I caught myself and laughed. "All right. No assumptions. You tell me."

"I'll tell you a funny thing. The best salesman on my staff is the most unprepossessing guy. He's quiet, low-keyed and a very sensitive human being—and what a salesman!"

Fascinated, I asked, "But why? What quality has he got?"

"Ah, he has one quality that I wish every man working for me had. He is able to put himself in the customer's shoes. He gets inside him. He knows what makes him tick."

"You mean he has *empathy*?"

"Empathy, *shmempathy*! He instinctively feels for people. He understands the client, and he

188

automatically knows the right moment for a hard sell, the right moment for a soft sell, when to push and when to keep his mouth shut. If that's what you call empathy, I'll buy it. What that man has makes him my most powerful salesman. I tell you, if he ever combines it with push and ambition, I'm going to have to watch out for my own job."

Empathy and aggression. They make a good pair, but empathy by itself is a fine coping tool. The ability to understand someone so well that you feel as they feel gives you an enormous amount of power over them. It works in corporate dealings, in labor mediation, in all forms of selling and buying, in all areas of business, but also on a personal level. You don't have to agree with someone in order to understand them.

In the family, the parent in empathy with his child can overcome the generation gap. He can understand how important it is for his child to look like the other kids, to wear the same hairstyle and clothes, to talk like them, or to rebel and insist on doing things his own way. The more you understand all these feelings, the more power you have in the relationship.

The same is true of the teacher in empathy with her students. I know of one young woman who taught in a ghetto school. Although she and her students were both black, she came from a middle class home, and there seemed no way she could bridge the gap between them. "Things got to the point where I was ready to quit," she confessed. "I had a lot to give those kids, but how can you give anything to children who won't trust you, who talk a different language and live a different life?"

"The last straw came when I arrived in class one

morning and saw Roy, one of my most recalcitrant pupils, spraying the blackboard with a paint can. I walked up and grabbed his arm, and I was just about to pour out all the concentrated venom of the entire term when the door opened and in walked the principal.''

"Having a bit of trouble?" he asked me, staring at Roy and the spray can and then at the blackboard. He was licking his chops at the idea of punishing a troublemaker. I could hear all the students holding their breath, and then, just as I was about to tell the principal all, I was suddenly struck with an inspiration.''

"I smiled and said, 'Oh, no! No trouble at all. Roy is helping me show the other students how hard it is to remove grafitti. He helped me spray the blackboard, and now we're going to call for volunteers to scrape it off. It's really a lesson in civics.'

"It was also a lesson in something else. By the time the principal left, surprised and suspicious, but unable to do anything, I had won Roy and the class over. We suddenly understood each other. There was a lot of giggling as we cleaned up, but I was a heroine to them, and the understanding, the empathy between us gave me the strength I needed. You know, I'm still at that school, and I wouldn't leave it for the world!''

The empathy she had developed helped her cope with that class, but it wasn't a quality that she pulled out of a hat. It had always been a part of her make-up, even though it had been obscured by the economic differences between her and her pupils. Almost everyone has some degree of empathy. In some of us it's well developed and in others it's

190

dormant, but each of us can strengthen that sense of empathy. We can all learn to see the world through other people's eyes.

The ability to understand how another person sees a particular situation, or, more important, how he *feels* about that situation, will often be your key to changing or dominating it. In the business world or in the personal world, empathy gives you an edge.

Reality depends, in part, on how you view the world, but it also depends on how others view it. Empathy gives you a firmer grasp on reality and lets you see all sides of a situation. You may not agree with the other person, but at least with empathy, you will understand his viewpoint. If he is a friend, the understanding will increase the friendship. If he is a stranger, it may help develop a friendship, and if he is an opponent, the understanding you gain from empathy will give you an advantage over him.

Putting It All Together

We have presented some of the most important coping tools in this chapter, but there are many more available as well as a great variety of coping techniques and styles. Almost any problem or situation can be managed by a dozen different approaches, and diffferent people use different methods.

We have to realize that the same coping technique doesn't work for every situation. What was successful last week in coping with your husband may not work this week when you're coping with your child.

Flexibility is probably the most valuable of the coping tools, and blended with assertion it can start you on the climb to power. But the person who adds empathy to flexibility and aggression and stirs in a dollop of reason is not only able to cope with power, but also with powerful people.

8

IMAGE PROJECTION

Dressing for Dinner

"Some years ago," Jerry told me, "I closed a sensational deal and came out with a big bundle of cash. My wife Martha and I decided to have a fling, to do it up right. Go to Europe on the *S. S. France*—and go first-class!"

I said enviously, "It must've been great."

"Great? It was incredible! Five days of the stuff of which dreams are made. I tell you—the food, the service—that first-class dining room was four stars, the ultimate, and you know, we had to dress for dinner every night. Man, there's something about getting decked out in evening clothes that changes you. Martha and I would walk down the staircase into the jazzy dining room, and we felt like we were two of the beautiful people."

"No kidding?"

"Let me tell you, when you're all dressed up like that you walk differently, you move differently and above all you feel different. You're somebody, somebody important. There's a sense of—of power. Now I know why rich folk used to dress for dinner. The image you project is a wonderful boost to your ego."

"Well, they've taken the *France* out of service, but you don't need an ocean liner to dress for dinner."

Jerry tried to answer, and began to laugh. I waited until he stopped, then asked, "What's so funny?"

"I'll tell you. You say we don't need the *France* to dress for dinner. That's what Martha and I thought when we got back to Omaha. We both talked it over and decided, what the hell. Why not dress for dinner at home, create a little fancy atmosphere? One night when the kids had something doing at school, Martha set the table with our best china and silver, and I put on my tux while she got into one of the gowns she had bought for the trip and . . ."

"And poof, you were both beautiful people!" I laughed. "Did it work?"

Jerry grinned sheepishly. "I was just uncorking the wine when the doorbell rang. I couldn't imagine who it could be, and Martha said, 'Don't answer it!" but I said, 'Hell, they'll see the lights.' So I went to the door and it was the Fischers, Bud and Natalie. They'd just dropped by!

"Bud looked at me and said, "What's up? Why the monkey suit?' and Natalie said, 'You both look so lovely. I like your gown, Martha. Very snazzy. Oh dear, we've come at a bad time, I guess we should've called, but we were in the neighborhood . . .'

"I was embarrassed. I didn't want to admit we had dressed up like this just for dinner at home, so I said quickly, 'It's a party. An old friend—his daugther was just married and . . .' then Martha jumped in with 'A formal reception, you know.'

" 'Well, have a wonderful time,' Natalie started

to say, and in barged our two kids. The school affair had been called off. 'Hey Mom, Dad, what's up?'

" 'It's a party, darlings.' My wife was quick to answer. 'We're on our way out. There's a stew on the stove for you and the table is set. Dad and I were just having a glass of wine before we left.' "

Jerry started to chuckle. "What a night! We drove around laughing hysterically for a half hour, then we went downtown and had dinner in one of the fanciest restaurants, feeling so out of place in our get-up that we didn't enjoy a mouthful. I tell you, it was the last time we tried to dress for dinner!"

By Their Clothes You Shall Know Them

The basic reason behind "dressing for dinner" is image projection. It was once a favorite pastime of the upper classes in Europe and America, and it faded away in the 30s, perhaps as an aftermath of the Depression. The image projected by evening dress is one of wealthy, luxury and power. To many wealthy people it began to seem immoral, and even dangerous, to project luxury when so many people were starving. Even if their personal wealth was unaffected, they cut back in an attempt to project spartan concern. There were, of course, small pockets of wealth that continued to flaunt their good fortune, but gradually, in the years that followed, the custom almost faded away.

It still hangs on here and there, in the first-class section of the ocean liner, the *Queen Elizabeth II*, at occasional wealthy estates here and abroad, in some resorts and at formal dinners—but generally these are anomalies. Sometimes their absurdity will be pointed out by someone like Woody Allen who will turn up at a formal occasion wearing tennis shoes with a tuxedo.

But even this is a calculated act of image projection, a way of saying, "I am powerful enough to stand custom on its head, to dress in a ridiculous fashion for a very formal event. In its way, it is as studied a gesture as the very proper outfits of the society men who match patent leather shoes to their evening clothes.

We dress for a multitude of reasons, ranging from protection against the weather to moral, religious and social mores. Not the least of these reasons is image projection. In part we dress to project an image, to show the world who we are, what we are, how important and powerful, how in tune with the times or how modest we are. Our clothes make a statement about us. In my friend Jerry's case, as he walked down the stairs to the dining room on the *France*, his clothes said, "I am a man of substance, cultured, one of a very elite group."

But clothes can make an equally important statement when they say, *I'm poor* or *I'm radical* or *I'm against the establishment*. Last spring I was taking a walk through a big city park during the lunch hour, indulging in my favorite pastime of people watching. At one point I saw a sloppily dressed young man ambling along. He wore jeans, a T-shirt and a pair of jogging shoes. A young woman came towards him, evidently on her lunch break from a nearby office. She was very pretty and had on a light grey suit, a white blouse, high heels and nylons on a pair of shapely legs.

The young man gave her a disinterested glance

and passed by. A few yards behind her was another young woman in jeans, a faded workshirt and sneakers. The young man's eyes lit up. He made some remark as he passed her. She laughed, looked back, and he turned and began to walk with her.

I watched them go up the park path together, wondering at the inexplicable taste of some people. The girl he had ignored was very lovely. The one he had decided to pick up was, in my eyes, a slob.

A psychiatrist friend of mine laughed when I told him about this incident. "What you don't understand," he said, "is that you witnessed a lesson in communication. The well dressed young woman was making a very definite statement about herself. Her clothes said, among other things, *I am a member of the establishment.* The young man was saying just the opposite with his jeans and T-shirt. He understood the girl's statement instantly, and had no interest in her. But when he saw another girl saying just what he was saying, his interest was aroused, and obviously so was hers. It was a case of a meeting of minds.

"I am also sure that your lovely young woman in her proper suit would have turned the heads of a half dozen young businessmen before she got out of the park. We dress to make a statement, all of us. Look at yourself. What do you wear for a business appointment? A suit and tie? For a walk in the park? Slacks and a sweater? To attend a symphony, a rock concern, to go out jogging? Each outfit says something about you to the people you associate with."

"Not jogging," I protested. "There I dress for convenience."

He shook his head. "Perhaps *you* do, or think you do, but then watch your fellow joggers.

There's an *in* style of running shorts, an *in* brand of shoes, an *in* sweatshirt—each says I'm in the know. I belong to the now generation. Each makes a statement, each projects an image."

Sometimes the image projected is a subtle one. My friend Jerry, talking about his memorable trip on the *France* said, "A funny thing—all of us dressed up in the evening for dinner and afterwards, but even in first-class, there were two classes."

"What do you mean, two classes?"

"Well, there was my class. Martha and I aren't rich. Oh, I'm well-off, but I could only afford that trip because I had a small windfall. Traveling like that isn't my usual style. When we outfitted ourselves, I bought the very latest tux. And Martha bought a few sharp evening dresses. We both wanted to look good, and you know, on shipboard we did look good—along with about two-thirds of the first-class passengers."

"What about the other third?"

"That's the point. Our clothes were smart and new, but I noticed that their clothes were—how can I put it?—dowdy. That's the word for it. The women's dresses looked as if they were picked up on a second-hand rack. Like the men's clothes, they were expensive, you could tell that, but just a bit—well, dated."

"That's puzzling, isn't it? You wouldn't expect that sort of dowdiness on such an expensive trip."

"That's just the point. I got chummy with one of the officers, and he assured me that those people were just as rich as the rest, maybe even richer, but they had old money, money that had been in the family for generations. Now he claimed that people with old money have a different dress code, as if they deliberately try to look a bit shabby. They act as if it's in poor taste to wear new and stylish clothes. You know what, if we ever again cross by boat, Martha says she's going to the local Salvation Army thrift shop to outfit herself." Jerry laughed. 'With the price of ocean liner travel, she'll have to!"

Jerry had shrewdly put his finger on one of the basic differences between the *nouveau riche* and the old, established upper class. The newly rich, unused to the money they have acquired, feel that they must use it to show off their wealth. New automobiles, homes, stereos, swimming pools, furs—all the symbols of wealth are proudly displayed. They work hard to project an image of affluence.

The older wealth adopts a slightly worn look to show an indifference, even a contempt for money. Their image says, "It's always been available. It's no special thing. We can afford the older cars, the old-fashioned houses, the clothes from another season (the finest clothes money can buy, but never flamboyant). We are not interested in the trappings of success, because we've arrived a long time ago."

Dressing Down

There is a movement among young people (and nowadays young has been stretched up into the forties; in fact, I know men and women in their fifties and sixties who look askance at the idea that they might be considered middle-aged or even older!) to achieve just what people with older wealth have achieved, the ability to look worn, a bit frayed or downright shabby. I know well-to-do writers who wear worn jeans with a shirt and tie and jacket, an outfit also worn by Senator Lowell Weicker for a recent formal television interview. Senator Weicker comes from "old money" and dressed for the occasion, casual with a slightly rumpled look. However, he wears the "look" well, and seems comfortable in his attire.

Some of the writers I know get their jackets from the better thrift shops, even if their shirts and ties are made by Hathaway and Pierre Cardin. However, I don't imagine that Senator Weicker spends his off-congressional hours prowling second hand shops of the nation's capital. One writer friend confided to me that "Thrift shop jackets have that instant work look, and if you search carefully, you can come up with one with a *Brooks Brothers* or *Saks Fifth Avenue* label. A good tweed with leather patches, now that's real class."

The jeans-jacket-and-tie look, a studied carelessness that also projects contempt for convention, is closely linked to the jeans and workshirt look. It too states, "I am above rules and regulations about clothes. The clothes I wear aren't important, but I am. Notice me, I don't have to conform."

This type of "dressing down" is equivalent to the Woody Allen sneakers-with-a-tuxedo look. It makes a number of statements:

> "I am not locked into contemporary attitudes about what is proper and improper."
> "I am successful and/or powerful enough to dress for comfort and not for appearance."
> "I am contemptuous of success and the money it brings with it."

On the other end of the image projection scale,

novelist Philip Roth in his book *The Ghost Writer* has his protagonist tell of visiting an internationally famous grand old literary man at his New England country home. Everything is slightly primitive, the weather snowy and cold, and the protagonist wears the rough, warm clothing suitable for the occasion. The Grand Old Man, however, appears in a business suit, a tie, a shirt and polished shoes. He *dresses up* in a *down* situation to show, in reverse fashion, his contempt for convention.

The major trouble with dressing down is that it very rapidly becomes popular, and the "look" is picked up by the majority. More and more men begin to "dress down," and jeans become a hot-selling item.

Local entrepreneurs, quick for a shot at the main chance, begin to market jeans, and all at once they are no longer work clothes. We suddenly have designer jeans, imported jeans, the baggy look, and on and on. Their price skyrockets as they become the *in* thing. Everyone wears them and they are best-sellers in the rag trade. We even get tailored denim suits for the man or woman who likes a certain formality in clothes but still wants to say in the mainstream of fashion.

Originally, in the 60s, Levi jeans, denim shirts, work boots and long hair were a statement of rebellion by our youth. It was a deliberate break with convention. The clothing said, "We don't want your dirty war, your trappings of power, your crew-cuts, shirt, tie and suit, your dresses and high heels, your double standards of morality." But alas, rebellion only works when there is no profit in it. The denim generation saw their symbols of rebellion taken over by the fashion industry and they began to look for something else. For a while it was painter's pants, farmer's overalls, carpenter's pants and then finally they discovered second-hand clothing. Inevitably, the designers caught up again and started turning out new clothes that looked like Mom's housedresses from the 30s. Second-hand Rose and Roger threw in the sponge, grew up, joined the establishment, exchanging their Levi's for Sassoons, their workboots for Fryes.

Remember my friend Alvin, in the first chapter? The guy who boned up on dressing for power, and then was left with egg on his face when he was interviewed by the executive in jeans and sneakers? He discovered that true power allows a man to cut through all the established dress codes and wear what he pleases. This executive was a powerful man for a very simple reason. He owned the company. It was not a corporation or part of a conglomerate. He didn't have to answer to a higher-up or to a Board of Directors. Nowadays it is unusual to find a business owned by one man, and it was just my friend Alvin's luck that he picked one when he applied for a job.

The Corporate Image

Some while back I was asked to address a seminar at a large data processing convention on *Body Language in a Sales Situation*. In the course of the seminar, I talked of image projection and asked why none of the dozen women in the room were wearing pants. They all had on either suits or skirts and blouses; there were no dresses and no pants suits. Was it corporate policy? I wondered.

One of the women told me that they had all attended a seminar a week before on *Dressing for Power*. The man who conducted it insisted that no woman in business should wear either a dress or pants. According to him, the only acceptable dress for women were skirts with either a jacket or a blouse and medium heels. The colors had to be black, navy or grey with a white blouse. The shoes had to be pumps in navy or black!

It was amazing to me that all the women had accepted these arbitrary rules about clothes and colors. I could have gone along with a "neat look," "no frills" or "businesslike outfit," but such rigid dictates of color and style seemed foolish. Yet this type of advice is constantly given and after a while, accepted not only by working men and women, but also by the big corporations themselves.

I did some research for a corporation that has a rigid dress code. Their men must wear business suits, no tweeds, no jackets and slacks, and the women are expected to dress very discretely with dark colors and simple lines. When I questioned an executive of the firm, I was told that there was a logic to their policy. "We project a corporate image, a no-nonsense image of stability and solidity. It tells our customers they can count on us, and it's extremely important in terms of public relations.

"In a giant corporation like ours," he went on, "a corporation which must exude confidence and security, the projected image also tells the public we hire a neat, competent and businesslike worker, the kind you can trust to be sensible and level-headed. You can trust him and, by implication, you can also trust the company."

When I seemed unconvinced, he went on earnestly. "Now you take a big city boutique that sells to young people. You'll find their salesmen wearing long hair and far-out clothes. They are trying to create a *with-it* image, not stability like us, but a *now generation* look. Well, maybe you think working under those conditions is freer, but let me tell you this. The salesman in that boutique who comes to work in a grey flannel suit and tie will be under the same pressure to conform and change as our corporate worker who tries to dress against the corporate image."

The problem with any corporation's rigid dress code is that it tends to promote a corresponding rigidity in thinking. In big business, management now understands that it needs innovative, imaginative and original people. The corporate workers who are trained to conform in thought as well as clothes are of little value when the corporation starts to hunt for new talent. As a result, management frequently goes outside its own organization to recruit.

When I suggested this to the corporate executive he shrugged. "You're right, and it *is* a problem. But you know, we always have a few mavericks who refuse to fit into the corporate image. They are free thinkers in clothes and ideas, and sometimes they get fired for just that reason. But if they resist the corporate stifling and still hang on, they have a terrific power base. They made a reputation for themselves in the firm, and management becomes aware of them and searches them out when it needs bright, talented *thinkers*."

He shook his head ruefully. "In a sense, our only corporate salvation is to advance these people, and if our personnel manager is on the ball, he singles them out. We don't despise mavericks, but we don't take every kook who comes down the pike! They must have talent, plenty of talent!"

The Masks We Wear

Clothes are one aspect of image projection, but there are many others. Hair style is important here. The Beatles proved that to America, and lately, when Farah Fawcett became popular, she proved it again by inspiring literally thousands of young and old imitators. Women all over the country bleached and cut and set their hair, and came out of the driers as sparkling clones of Farah. They all hoped to project the same image that worked so well for her, hoping that some of her power of sexual attraction would rub off on them.

In men, long hair and beards were the image projections of youth a few years back. Now hair is getting shorter and beards are fading. Moustaches are the latest expressions of being with it. Sometimes a single earring in a man signals a *macho* image. For many men *macho* is equated with power. But in other areas the same earring signals homosexuality.

The homosexual and the *macho* image are rarely far apart and understandably so. The more masculine the image projected, the more attractive a homosexual is to other homosexuals, and so we have the phenomenon of "leather bars," where admittance depends on jeans and leather jackets and boots and all the trappings we have always associated with motorcycle gangs and the like.

But all of us project an image of one sort or another, and we depend on that image for a feeling of power and importance. The old cliche, "Clothes make the man or woman" has a good core of truth to it.

It is for this reason that dressing properly for a job interview makes sense. Of course, we do want to make a good impression on whoever interviews us. It's stupid to dress flamboyantly, sloppily or out of keeping with regulations of the company. But over and above any impression we may make on our prospective employer, there is the impression we make on ourselves, the extent to which the image we think we project strengthens our feelings about ourselves.

Sometimes we try to keep the true image locked away. We seek privacy by wearing a mask, and sometimes the mask can be our own face. The simplest mask is the non-committal look, the face without expression. Children learn this very early, sometimes in self-defense when the show of any emotion would expose them to a hostile adult world.

As they grow older, children learn that the expressionless face gives away the fact that they are masking. Some sort of expression becomes a better mask. A smile is the most common one, and it can hide unhappiness, anger or disappointment. Some people smile constantly, no matter what turmoil is going on inside them. But as helpful as a smile may be in masking, a grim look is also effective. It can mask joy and happiness and elation.

Many of us go beyond expression. Women use makeup to exaggerate and change their features, to emphasize their lips, make their eyes larger, give life to their cheeks and color to their skin. Men use bronzing lotions to simulate a tan and mask their winter pallor. Men also use hair as a mask. A full moustache can cover a baby face and present a virile aspect to the world. A beard may conceal a weak chin, add a touch of glamour or a bit of cool, while a hairpiece hides signs of age.

When we stop to think about it, masking is a universal device. Politeness, respect, even homage are all elaborations of masking. We mask constantly to get along in business, at home, with lovers, friends and family. We mask to hide our inner feelings, to keep our inner selves from being exposed.

There is nothing wrong with masking—its universality should tell us that—as long as it's kept within reasonable limits. In fact, showing our true feelings is often considered wrong and selfish. Boys are taught to mask fear with a brave aspect, girls to hide distaste with flirting. Teachers mask to their students to encourage them to grow and develop.

A teacher explained this to me the only way she could function. "What else can I do? Tell them the truth? Their work is awkward, ungrammatical, childish. If I told them that, it would be destructive. No, my job is to encourage my students, so I mask my feelings, and praise them for trying. That's how they grow."

A parent does the same thing with a young child, an impatient salesman with a reluctant client, a worker with his boss. They all learn to mask for either survival or to help others.

Too much masking, of course, can be harmful. Then we begin to suppress feelings that need to come out in the open. We build up anger and hostility, and yet, taking off the mask is a difficult process.

"I am not at all sure," a young businessman, Milt, told me, "that human beings can live comfortably without masks."

"Why do you say that?" I asked him.

"I've been there and back. Like I went to this week-long encounter group up in the mountains, and once I got into it it was wonderful, a complete new way of seeing and feeling. Oh, at first we all resisted it. Some of the men were just there for kicks, and some women were too uptight. But after the second day we began to get it all together—like we shook off our defenses and got to know each other, deep down without masking.

"It was heavy, man, but one by one our masks dropped. We all became very close, and when I came back to work the next Monday, I was fully prepared to be open and honest, and then, Bam! There it was!"

"What?"

"Well, I had to start right in by lying to customers about why their orders hadn't gone out. I couldn't be honest and tell them someone had forgotten. Then I had to cover up some mistakes my assistant had made while I was gone. Usually he's pretty good, but he has trouble functioning alone. I couldn't louse him up, could I? I didn't have the heart to tell our art department how rotten one of their layouts was, I know that the artist who worked on it is going through a bad scene at home, so I had to find some excuse for not using it. I had to hide my anger at how late he was when I talked to our printer, or I might not have gotten the job done at all, and so it went, and I was right back where I was before, lying and covering up to get along. You can't drop your mask in this world. You just can't!"

The Hired Brain

But in the business world, as Milt said, masking is the order of the day. I talked to a number of top corporate men about this, and they were unanimous in agreeing on the importance of masking. "You get along in the corporate world," one told me, "by masking what you really feel and comforming to success."

"What exactly does that mean?"

"I'll tell you. You act like the top men in business. You dress like them, think like them, and ally yourself with them—or you mask everything you really feel in order to give that impression. That's how you get power, by getting to be known as a sound person."

"What about ability and experience?" I asked.

"I assume that you have both, or you'd never get into the top echelon. Once you've made it, you can stay if you can be part of the team, if you can conform, if you can hide all your doubts and indecisions. You pick up certain techniques of power. You learn to speak in a rich, assured voice. You talk with confidence and never say no. Get someone else to do that. You've heard of *yes men*. Well, they're important to a man in power, but so are *no men*. Hire someone to say no for you. Let him be the Cassandra. Your best bet is a modulated maybe. Be a *maybe man*, optimistic but practical. Use expressions such as, *I really want to think about this,* or *Let's kick it around a bit.*"

"Never confuse your superior with details. When you make an instant decision, play act a bit. Delay letting anyone know what you've decided so that it looks as if you've thought it through carefully. You see, you want to come across as a stable person. And one final piece of advice—don't appear too smart. Remember appearance is often more important than substance. Cultivate a warm, engaging smile."

"I can't believe that all of that leads to success and power," I protested.

He corrected me quickly. "I never said that! What you call *all of that* is what comes *after* you've obtained success and power. First you have to have the power. I was just giving advice on how to behave once you're in the catbird seat. Getting there is a different story. All the play acting in the world won't give you power. My point is, you have to have power to play act."

I asked a number of others about the connection between knowledge and power. "Are the men in power the men who know the most? Or, to put it another way, do the smartest men rise to power?"

One man who understood the answer is someone I respect both for his business ability and his knowledge. "We all like to think that knowledge pays off," he said thoughtfully, "that powerful, wealthy men must be smart as well. But you know, C. Wright Mills, the sociologist, put it very well. He said if we figure that those who get power must be smart, we are saying that power is knowledge. If we say those who make money are smart, we're saying wealth is knowledge. The point is, we don't think of knowledge as an idea. We see it as a means of getting wealth and power. We like to think that the smart guy gets ahead.

"But if you took the hundred smartest men in this country and the hundred most powerful men, how many do you think would be in both groups?"

"Very few."

"Very few indeed. Now it wasn't always like that. In the eighteenth century powerful men studied, and smart men were often in power. But today that's no longer true. Instead, men in power surround themselves with smart people. Your man with the smarts tends to be a consultant, not a businessman. He may be a speechwriter or an advisor, not a politician."

"The smartest politicians and businessmen are smart enough to realize that they aren't expected to make decisions, so they hire brains, public relations men, ghost writers, secretaries, researchers, administrative assistants—and after a while, being smart, being knowledgeable, being an intellectual is something to be ashamed of, to look down on. Smart men are the ones for hire. The true men of power can always buy them. Why cultivate knowledge?"

There is another aspect of power that seems unique to this century, and that is popularity. Someone with "star" quality, someone with "charisma" can become truly powerful. Entertainers such as Sinatra and Presley swayed millions with their charisma and ended up with popularity power. Movie stars, singers, talk show hosts, athletes are all media heroes and have the power to set trends.

Here, while power goes with charisma, there is little connection between charisma and knowledge. These super stars may be intelligent, but the most popular among them have the least amount of knowledge. They may not even know how to handle their own lives. We see this again and again in their involvement with drugs or drink, or broken marriages and swollen but battered egos, and sometimes in a drive towards suicide.

But they too are able to buy knowledge, to turn to PR people, to writers, managers and consultants to build images that will present acceptable fantasies to the public. In one way this is another evidence of masking to hide a personal weakness and give the aura of power to a popular person.

Sometimes, paradoxically, the fantasy presented to the public stresses a weakness. *How I found true love. How I licked the drug habit. How I overcame alcohol. How I held my marriage together. How I made my comeback.* But the emphasis is always on overcoming the weakness, and the connection is made between power and the ability to rise above any problem.

Yet with all of this, such power is usually ephemeral. The public is very fickle. What it embraces today, it forgets tomorrow. Let a top football player have a bad season, and he's out of favor. Let a star have one or two box office flops, and she's quickly forgotten. In many cases the real power behind these charismatic heroes is the media, the press agent, the manager. Once the star is no longer a moneymaker, the hired brain turns to some other, newer power, for his own survival.

9

THE POWER PACKAGE

Packaging People

The concern with outward appearance, with show, with the "packaging" of people, is evident in all of the books about power. One of the most popular books speaks of the physical signs that spell out strength; the immobile face, the direct gaze, quiet hands. In a bland return to all the discredited ideas of the nineteenth century, the author notes that a large face with at least one overpowering feature such as General DeGaulle's nose helps create a sense of power.

If any one lasting discovery about personality has come out of modern psychology, it is the fact that there is no connection whatever between our outer appearance and our inner selves. The smartest people can have the lowest brows, the strongest can have the weakest chins or noses. There is simply no connection between face and personality, and yet again and again we are told about such connections!

This same best-selling book on power concentrates to an overwhelming degree on the packaging of people to ensure success. Starting with the jutting nose, hooded eyes, and prominent cheekbones, the author builds up, feature by feature, his own idea of a "portrait of power." He pushes his theme a bit further by describing motions of power—how to plant your feet firmly, how to move powerfully, how to dominate a conversation.

None of this is done from the point of feedback, the concept that acting like this might make you feel more powerful. The idea behind it all is packaging. This is how powerful people are packaged. Let the fairy godmother of success wave her magic wand and give you the same wrappings and presto! You too will be powerful. If only it worked.

The writer of the most popular book about power talks of the most powerful office in the business world, the corner one, and goes on to tell you how to stand in a position of power at a party (in a corner of course) and then he advises how to play all the games of power. He ends the book with a number of power "rules," notable among them the last rule, "Don't make waves!"

It all adds up to a wonderful manual on packaging people. Wrap the man or woman in all the trappings of power and teach him or her all the moves of power with the added caution, "Don't make waves." If you keep the wrappings of power and not stir anyone up enough to want to peek behind the wrappings, it is just possible that no one will ever notice that there is nothing there, that under the tailored suit, the expensive silk tie and white shirt, and strong face with its jutting nose, and powerful moves and games, the corner office and all the rest, there is just an empty, frightened little person dreading discovery.

Looking Out for You-Know-Who

If the packaging is all there is, and once you've taken off the ribbons and paper and nothing substantial remains, all is not lost, another writer on power assures us. He speaks of all the wrong zones we get lost in, and gives us a formula for filling the empty package. The formula contains enough bits of truth to be convincing, but it also contains a troubling premise. Focus on your own wants, your own desires and needs. Love yourself enough and you will expand to fill that empty box.

There is no doubt that self-worth and self-respect are important. Without them we are crippled. We are deprived not only of power but also of any real intimacy or love. There is also no doubt that we must think highly of ourselves before we can think highly of anyone else, but the answer is not an excessive involvement with self. We each exist in terms of other people, in conflict with others, in love with others, being helped by others and helping others. None of us is alone. We could not exist alone for very long.

The book that would lead us to power by cutting out all our wrong zones would also lead us to a narcissistic involvement with ourselves. The author tells us he has practiced what he preaches and has become a coast-to-coast celebrity by putting himself first and promoting himself on television and radio across the country. He has become, a blurb for the book states, like his own ideal character, and in the final chapter he tells us what his ideal character is.

Among other things, he wastes no time in

wishing that things were otherwise. He is a non-worrier. He lives in the present. He puts a high premium on privacy and is adamant about his freedom. He doesn't look for the approval of others, and he accepts himself without complaint—and so on and on.

It surprises me that this idealized man is put forth as a paragon of power. The man who doesn't wish that things were otherwise, who doesn't worry and lives only in the present is a man with a very weak grasp of reality. We only have to pick up the daily newspaper to understand that there is plenty to worry about.

But then, this man who has freed himself from his wrong zones has no need to worry. His need for privacy and freedom, his disinterest in anyone else's approval and his acceptance of himself are all strong enough—or so he thinks.

Like so many other books, the "zone" idea in a subtle way stresses non-involvement. *Don't worry about what other people think, go out and do your own thing, do what you want to do, be yourself.* We belong to the "Me Generation" and are concerned with ourselves to the exclusion of everyone else. We neglect our children to find ourselves, and then complain when our children neglect us.

We turn Shakespeare's "To thine own self be true" around to mean "Being our own true selves." But in doing so we lose the enormous power that comes from involvement. We break up the family and put our old folks away in homes, and then yearn for the good old days and the extended family. We turn inward to improve ourselves, always ourselves, and then wonder at the lack of power that that self possesses.

216

Still another book urges us deeper into an obsession with the self. This tells us to look out for you-know-who, the most important person, and it gives us a series of exercises on how to do it. This was written by the same man who taught us how to intimidate others, and he makes a strong case for being *rationally selfish,* and *involved with pleasure of the present*. Here too, the message is selfishness as a key to power.

If any one of us were to follow the directions in all these books, and follow them exactly, would we achieve power? Perhaps selfish power, but by nature human beings are not selfish animals. We cannot be happy alone, and learning to be involved only with ourselves is the quickest road to loneliness.

Perhaps, when the trappings of power are taken away, when the package is opened, there will be something there, but whatever it is will be so turned in on itself that it will be the human equivalent of a black hole, collapsed inward by an overwhelming gravity of selfishness.

Epilogue

POWER WITH CLASS

Creative Power

This book is subtitled *How to Get Power With Class,* and for class you can substitute good taste, dignity, involvement with others, love and affection and an absence of game-playing. You can get power with class, but the first thing you must do is change your conception of power. You must discard the idea that power is merely a manipulative something that will allow you to intimidate others to get them to do what you want. You must learn to see power principally as a creative force.

The most powerful people are those who do things, and that applies on every level from the worker to the artist, the writer to the banker, the cook to the chairman of the board. In every field, those who do things best are most powerful. With this in mind, you can set out to avoid all those unpleasant little power games that do little besides feed the ego.

Game-playing to get power and to consolidate it is used in business, as we saw in the first chapter, and it's also used in the home in interpersonal relationships between husband and wife, between lover and loved, between parents and children and even among friends. The games of helplessness and martyrdom are old stand-bys in the family struggle for power. But by their very nature, even when they work, such tactics erode the power they get.

Before you go after, or demand power, you must be able to handle it, you must understand your own power profile. Will you be happy with power, or are you the kind of person who wants no part of it? There is no disgrace to being happy without power. Some of us are not born to lead. We may be followers or independents, but we must know what we are. Too many problems arise when we strike out in the wrong direction, when we go after a position or relationship that doesn't suit us.

In Chapter Two the tests and questions gave you some insight into your own desires for power or your degree of aggression. They will tell you whether you should go after power or be indifferent to it.

Very well, you've tested yourself and decided that you're not only comfortable with power, but you need power to make yourself more comfortable. The next step is to understand power and its sources.

The apparently simple definitions of creative and manipulative power become more complicated as we understand the ramifications of coercive power and legitimate power, reward power and group power. It becomes apparent that the question is only partly, "Can I handle power?" The other part of the question is "What kind of power should I go after? What part of the power spectrum is right for me?"

Power, in all its overt forms, has been a male province throughout history. Before the twentieth century it was rare for a woman to rise to political power or the power of wealth unless she inherited the position. In most cases, power and men were linked. Women had to get their power through men, through manipulative games, by being the power behind the throne, rarely the power on it. In the family, until this century, women were completely powerless. Their only strength lay in managing things through their husbands or children.

Today, women are coming out of the power closet. They are beginning to use power openly and understand it and, in many cases, to hammer out techniques for dealing with it that are peculiarly feminine. But all the years of being powerless have taken their toll. When a woman does achieve power she often reacts with guilt and uneasiness. Have I the right to be powerful? Won't power take away my femininity, make me less of a woman? These are questions that every woman who struggles ahead has to face and answer.

Once you understand power's dangers and still want to get into the power struggle, you may still be crippled by your own power inadequacy. You may just not be a powerful person—and yet you may want and even need power to develop fully. You may also recognize the fact that you have something to contribute to the power elite, your own unique strengths and ideas. How do you get enough power to fight for power?

One way is through feedback. Simply stated, this means that if you act powerful, you will feel a bit more powerful inside yourself, and this in turn will allow you to act with even more power. A part of this feedback mechanism lies in your body language. If you walk tall and stand firm, you'll feel a bit taller, a bit firmer, and this will make it easier for you to act tall and firm with more conviction. The body language of power and metacommunication of power are two elements used by people in positions of power. Earlier in this book we pointed out that there are the trappings of power, the "packaging" that power comes in. It doesn't help to gift-wrap the person, if there is no power at the core. But if there is potential for power, appearance can exert a feedback, and that is one way to increase your own power.

The important factor here is to look at yourself realistically. All the trappings of power will do you no good if you haven't the potential of power. That's why the earlier question section in the book is so important. You must understand your own inner drives—or lack of them.

Risks, Stress and Reason

One of the rules of power is that it never comes to those who wait. If you want power, you must go after it. You have to be prepared to take a risk in order to achieve it. In general, the ability to risk goes hand in hand with the drive for power. The people who get ahead in the world are the same ones who take chances.

But along with risking there is responsibility. If you take a chance you must be prepared for the consequences. Quit your job for a better one and you must accept the possibility that the other job may not work out. If you risk your money on an investment, you should understand that it is just that—a risk—and you must be prepared if it doesn't pay off.

We risk on a personal level too. Every set of marriage vows is a risk taken by two people. Each gives up a certain freedom for marriage, hoping to gain more than is lost, but each must understand that there is a risk involved. And yet without these risks life would be intolerable. We would never move ahead.

One of the qualities that drives us to take risks is stress. A mild degree of stress similiar to anxiety is nature's way of keeping us alert and attentive. The stressed, anxious animal is the one that survives. Of course too much stress and too much anxiety can be harmful to man or beast, but a moderate amount of it will help a person to risk a bit more, to try a bit harder, to cope a bit better, to become a bit more powerful.

Coping is one of the skills that can make or break the struggle for power. First of all, there is the problem of coping with ways to get power, and even more essential, coping with power once we have it. One of the most useful tools to help you cope with the struggle for power and with power is aggression, or its more acceptable variant—assert-iveness.

Assertiveness can be learned, and if it is used wisely it can be a great aid in getting and using power. Assertiveness, like body language, acts in a feedback cycle. Act more assertively, and your spine will be stiffened a little, enough to make it easier the next time around.

Flexibility is almost as essential a coping tool as assertiveness in getting and keeping power. But in handling life in general, flexibility is even more important. The flexible man knows when to quit, as well as when to struggle ahead.

Another useful coping tool is reason, a three-sided prism. Reason is the quality that first impelled man to fit a bit of stone to a stick and hurl it at an animal. It gave him a power edge over his environment, an edge that he has been taking advantage of ever since.

Reason is made up of ambiguity, the ability to see that the world is more than black and white—is indeed all shades of grey. Objectivity is also a part of reason. This is the ability to step away from yourself and look at what you are doing without becoming emotionally involved. The third part of the prism of reason is discrimination, selecting the right decision, the one that will be best for you.

Another coping tool that can help us in our use of power is empathy, understanding another's point of view, putting yourself in someone else's shoes.

The feedback in body language, risking, and coping works to strengthen the power within you, to increase your inner strength so that you can use power correctly and get along with people who have power. The image you project also has a role in this complicated process. The way other people treat you depends, to a great degree, on the way they perceive you.

The middle-aged man who sets out to show the world a "with-it" image may only succeed in looking foolish. The woman who tries for sophistication may come across as vulgar. The young man who wants to be tough and *macho* may end up looking like a bully.

Before you can project respectability or strength

or worldliness or anything else, you have to understand your own essential nature, what elements make up your own true personality.

Self-understanding—that's the beginning of *power with class*!